PENGUIN BOOKS

WE WEREN'T LOVERS LIKE THAT

Navtej Sarna was born in Jalandhar, India. After studying Commerce and Law at Delhi University, he joined the Indian Foreign Service in 1980. He is presently the Spokesperson for the Foreign Office in Delhi and has earlier served as a diplomat in Moscow, Warsaw, Thimphu, Geneva, Tehran and Washington DC.

He has contributed short stories to the BBC World Service, *London Magazine* and to the anthologies *Signals* and *Signals 2*. His book reviews appear in the *Times Literary Supplement*, *Biblio* and other journals. In 1991, he published *Folk Tales of Poland*. This is his first novel.

We Weren't Lovers
Like That

Navtej Sarna

PENGUIN BOOKS

Penguin Books India (P) Ltd., 11 Community Centre, Panchsheel Park,
New Delhi 110 017, India
Penguin Books Ltd., 80 Strand, London WC2R 0RL, UK
Penguin Group Inc., 375 Hudson Street, New York, NY 10014, USA
Penguin Books Australia Ltd., 250 Camberwell Road, Camberwell,
Victoria 3124, Australia
Penguin Books Canada Ltd., 10 Alcorn Avenue, Suite 300, Toronto,
Ontario, M4V 3B2,Canada
Penguin Books (NZ) Ltd., Cnr Rosedale and Airborne Roads, Albany,
Auckland, New Zealand
Penguin Books (South Africa) (Pty) Ltd, 24 Sturdee Avenue,
Rosebank 2196, South Africa

First published by Penguin Books India 2003

Typeset in *Adobe Garamond* by SÜRYA, New Delhi
Printed at Thomson Press, Noida

To Avina,
who believed it could be done.

Acknowledgements

I owe more than I can say to my parents—my mother Surjit, who taught me to read the changing light of the seasons, and to my father Mohinder, whose gentle nudge pushed me to finish this book. I will have to live with the regret that I could not finish it quickly enough for him to see it in print.

I am indebted also to David Davidar at Penguin for pointing me in the direction of Ravi Singh. And a very special word of thanks to Ravi Singh who discerned, over beer at Berkeley, a book in the undergrowth of the first draft and then helped fashion it with amazing perception and patience.

Thanks also to all my friends, especially Nasser and Neeraj, for a thousand conversations that have enriched my life; to my sister Jaskiran, for keeping alive my associations with the once beautiful valley; and to my two dears Satyajit and Nooreen, for giving up so many weekends and still cheering heartily from the sidelines.

I regret picking
and not picking
violets.

—Anon

DELHI

1

I am leaving. Doing the one thing I feel I am still good at: running away. Towards the young green hills, a strange forgotten anticipation once again in my blood.

The city sleeps in the early morning as I throw my bag into the taxi. A driver and a younger man, both with saffron turbans on their heads—flat, hastily tied turbans—yawn their greetings, and their hands unconsciously smoothen their open beards. I am hoping they won't want to talk to me, ask where I'm going, when I'll be back. We drive through the deserted streets of Delhi. These streets have grown up with me. From cycle lanes they have become two, then four, some eight lanes, while I have lost my hair, changed my spectacles many times and gained several pounds around my waist. I can see people asleep on the pavements, in the shelter of bus stops, on stone benches, on wooden carts. Soon they will wake up and start selling things on these carts. All sorts of things that change with the seasons: peanuts heated by a little fire in a charred earthen pot, jamuns coated with salt that leave the mouth dry, boiled eggs cut in two and sold in the clouded light of a paraffin lamp. But for the moment, they sleep. The taxi skirts around Connaught Place, turns under the bridge and jerks to a halt in the parking lot outside New Delhi Railway Station.

I have seen this station on crowded summer nights when the

three-wheelers, taxis, cycle-rickshaws and tongas come together under the blue-white tube lights. Coolies with trunks and bedrolls rush up and down the worn staircases of the rusted pedestrian bridge that spans fourteen platforms, watched by the red and yellow revolving eyes of the weighing machines. Steel trolleys sell tea and biscuits and yellow cake on damp saucers. People fill water in plastic water bottles from the old stone water fountain. I have seen the bustle so often: people preparing for their journeys, dressed in kurta pyjamas and rubber chappals, their faces washed and scrubbed, their hair combed for the night, all going away, reaching somewhere else. Going back to their petty lives, petty jobs, petty relationships with wives, husbands, mothers-in-law. Attending weddings and births and funerals mindlessly.

But now, in the early morning, the platform is clean and almost quiet. Only a few beggars and a handful of passengers wait for the Shatabadi express to Dehradun.

'Sahib, coolie?'

I look at his wasted face, hanging in bulging bags, hard gray stubble scattered over his chin. I wonder why he calls me sahib. Maybe because of my clean cotton shirt and khaki trousers or my good walking shoes or the fact that I shave every morning. Or maybe he knows no better word. For him everybody on this platform is a sahib, anyone who can give him ten rupees.

I don't really need him. My bag is not too heavy; my reservation is in order, typed out on the chart in the centre of the platform: Aftab Chandra, Male-41, Wagon C-6, Seat 30—it says everything that is essential and nothing more. Yet I let him take my bag. With a fluid left-handed motion, he winds a piece of brown cloth on his head and puts my bag on it. His neck straightens up and he begins to walk heavily towards the train gliding in. He has grown old walking up and down these platforms. The whole world that lives on both sides of the crumbling walls of Delhi, on both banks of the ancient river, across the plain beyond and in the hills where the train will take me, has grown old. And the odour that rises from this ageing, bloated world sickens me. I have had enough of its meandering deceptions, of its wayward promises. Taking this train seems one way of getting my own back.

2

I turned forty at the turn of the century. I suppose that should have been an event by itself, a monumental conversation piece. Just that odd coincidence, for I can call it little else, should have been enough to get me invited to several turn-of-the-century parties where I could have been presented as something of a celestial oddity. What made things worse was that it was not just the end of the century but also of the millennium. So my turning forty was celebrated the world over. And it had all been in the planning for more than twenty years, from a time when I had no idea of what it meant to be forty, no feel at all for a reasonable bank balance, discreet reading glasses, flab around the middle, a mild drink habit, a sense of time slipping away. People had put away champagne in 1982, booked tables in Times Square in 1985 and bought tickets for rock concerts near the North Pole. Trips to the Galapagos Islands had been meticulously planned and fortunes spent for the privilege of staring at the moonlit Taj Mahal when the gong would finally make me forty. Just about everything—the stock market, psychosomatic disorders, the rising rate of murders, Y2K, angst, rage, depression, joy—was linked to my fortieth birthday. People made and lost fortunes in its anticipation, rock-stable marriages broke and long-lost lovers came together, drawn impulsively by a magic force.

When the moment finally came, I was watching television. And it wasn't particularly inspiring television either. They didn't quite know how to handle it. It is easy to pick out highlights and describe a year and I suppose they could have managed it even with a hundred years. They didn't have a hope with a thousand. Finally they gave up and began to show how the corks were popping all over the world as the sun went down. That the sun went down at different times made it all easier; the programmes could be stretched until everybody got sick of lights flashing, confetti floating, horns blaring, fireworks lighting up the sky.

I couldn't have given a damn if I had turned forty or eighty. I couldn't have possibly felt any worse. The world around me had begun to crumble in an uncontrollable sort of way. Everything that I touched seemed to slip away from my fingers. I had finally even stopped blaming everybody else and had begun to wonder whether it was somehow all my fault.

I suppose it was the beginning of my mid-life crisis. I had been waiting all my life, or at least half my life, for it. It comes, I am told, in different ways to different people: when someone's father dies; or after a sudden one-night stand. Or it can happen in the clinic of a suburban doctor who looks up from the blood report, takes off his half-moon spectacles and explains grimly that the patient's cholesterol and all other levels are far and way beyond the required limits and that he had better stop as of yesterday eating everything that he likes.

For me, it was a lost telephone diary.

It was an old diary that I had received several years ago for ordering a twelve-month subscription of a fortnightly news magazine. I should have actually let somebody in the office keep that diary. That would have been ethically correct. But there was something about it that was so old-world, so reliable—perhaps the gray cloth herringbone pattern that reminded me of my father's fifty-year-old overcoat—that I could not resist it. Let me confess here that I have never been able to resist items of stationery—transparent tape dispensers, plastic pencil sharpeners, little staplers, even smaller staple removers, multi-coloured highlighters, file covers, notebooks ... Three drawers of my writing table and an entire shelf in an old cupboard are full of such things. The staples have begun to rust and the highlighters and markers have long dried up but I have collected, hoarded them from wherever I could. From offices, shops, other people's writing desks ... In the beginning I used to spend money on these things. At twenty-two, on my first visit abroad, I spent a fortune in a stationery shop, buying airmail envelopes of a particular square shape and huge block notes of multicoloured paper. They still lie on my desk, happily unspent. Later I pursued my passion at less personal cost and have charmed, bludgeoned, cajoled these items away for my collection. So I took that diary, even though I had come to dislike the fortnightly for its not-even-a-pretense-about-it aping of American news magazines.

The diary was for my friends. Mere acquaintances would never make it there—I was very clear about that. It was only meant for people whom I would really write to, inspired by a certain light in the evening sky or by a recollection of a song. Or to whom I would place a call on an impulse even if they were half a world away, just to hear their voice. The addresses were chopped and changed along the years, the phone numbers became longer, e-mail addresses were added, names of husbands and wives and even children appeared in brackets. I could tell, perhaps better than they themselves could have, how their lives had changed. It had all been put down in my deliberately neat angular writing, the kind of writing I especially affect for filling in address books—three short lines in black with five-digit phone numbers; then scrawls in green felt pen, scratched out and finally entered again in blue ink, superseding all earlier entries. The diary had recorded it all, their movements from small towns to Delhi and Bombay, to rainy England or faraway big-time America. That diary was my ultimate response to the creeping world of electronic organizers and digital diaries and that latest foul thing called PDA. I wanted to have nothing to do with those. My friends belonged to another era and I thought my friendships were of a different, more durable kind.

And then, three days after Mina left, I went and lost it.

With it I lost whatever stability still remained in my life, the certainty of old memories, of faint associations lying like pressed flowers in my consciousness, the priceless (even more priceless as one gets older) link of a birthday card or new year greeting. It seemed that all the old faithfuls who I thought would always take my side, no matter what the odds, had, in one calculated, collective betrayal, deserted me. A Brutus-like team effort. Was it because over the fourteen years of our domesticity they had begun to like Mina more than me, having found her more organized, more confiding, more affectionate and altogether more sensible? Was that the reason they had chosen to leave me along with her?

Let me hand her this: in her own way, Mina tried to make it easy for me. Even on the day when she finally told me, once again, about her and Rajiv. It was the week before Diwali, when I usually try to take a day or two off, walk the bazaars, hang out in the verandas of the Indian Oil building and buy odds and ends. An occasional kurta in Khadi Bhandar, taking advantage of the October ten per cent discount; a pair of brown suede shoes; a new wallet from Kashmir handicrafts. Just a little personal festive indulgence that builds up gradually and nicely to the cautious recklessness of Diwali night when I play cards. I play with small but exciting stakes, doing the kind of things I never do in everyday life, chancing my arm, testing my luck, steeling my nerves, playing blind round after round, forcing those who have been dealt a better hand to bow out of the game. I never play cards except on Diwali; Diwali changes gambling to a ceremony.

Like when we used to play in the old days in my grandmother's house on two white sheets spread out on the red-and-black Mirzapuri carpet in the drawing room. The pile of chappals and sandals grew at the edge of the carpet as uncles and aunts and cousins came in one by one, making a big show of taking money out of their wallets, exchanging it for coins or counters, edging themselves modestly into the circle, asking the usual questions about the rules (Is 1-2-3 higher than King-Queen-Jack . . .?) that they asked every year to show that they were really not gamblers, you know. And then, as the inhibitions fell away and tea came around in glasses on round trays and the shuffling of the pack became more fluent, we felt the warmth of Diwali and thanked God that we were all together and it warmed my heart to see my grandmother smiling from a sofa, wrapped up in her cream Kashmiri shawl with its tiny red and green embroidered flowers, asking every now and then who was winning and who was losing.

Outside, on the balcony that overlooked the four-quartered park with the fountain and the low hedges and the new stone benches, one could smell the firecrackers and see the acrid smoke slowly cloud the candle-lit night. After Diwali, the sunlight would change its colour to a warm yellow and we would play cricket, matching our talents ball by ball with the heroic deeds being brought to us from the Test matches at Ferozeshah Kotla on a Philips transistor radio. I have tried to explain to Ankur the joy of listening to cricket commentary on that radio, the thrill of tuning it just right to hear the voices of Devraj Puri and Pearson Surita describing the shadows lengthening onto the pitch, to imagine, while sitting in that sunny park and mindlessly chewing blades of fresh grass, the exquisite beauty of Wadekar's late cut racing to the boundary or the devilish cunning of Chandra's googly trapping Barrington leg before on ninety-seven. But I don't think he ever got it. I cannot blame him; television killed all that.

In the years when we were in Dehradun, far away from my grandmother's warm circle on the red-and-black carpet, we would set up our own little circle, my father and mother, my sister and I, and play cards for a while, fulfilling a ceremony, while the crackers burst outside. Anars and bombs, whistles and hawais, phuljharis and chakkars on marble chipped floors and on the road and in stony backyards. And then the mithai would be cooked in a new utensil always bought by my mother on the day before Diwali, a strange fixation for a person who never insisted on anything else.

It was on such a day that Mina decided to tell me again about Rajiv.

The winter sun slanted down on our table, near the black pillar in the veranda of Triveni gallery. In summer we sat inside at our usual summer table, on low stools with embroidered cushions, but in winter we would wait for the veranda tables no matter how long it took. Below the veranda, in the open area that sometimes served as a stage, beyond the straggling green plants and the flowers in the brown pots, there was some sort of sale-cum-exhibition going on. People were walking around buying leather bags, kurtas, handmade paper.

'Aloo parathas and raita,' I told Kishen, the usual veranda waiter.

'Raita finish.' He did not look up, wiping the table needlessly in quick wide arcs.

'Make it kababs then.'

'The same,' said Mina, 'and water without ice.'

I watched her face and waited. I knew from the way she was looking beyond my head and the way her lips were pursed that she was lost in thought. The brown mole near her right eye, to which she used to match her brown lipstick, was twitching as it did when she was tense. I knew she wanted to say something. But this was not going to be just a fight. A fight could happen anywhere, in the bedroom or the kitchen or while walking around the house, closing windows, banging doors, straightening books on the shelves or the newspapers on the floor. It could go on in the car, pausing at red lights so that people in the next car did not hear the mutual bitching. A fight didn't mean that things were changing, it only meant that we were not happy with the way things were and that wasn't something very unusual. Most people I know are probably unhappy with the way things are. So life usually went on as we fought.

Mina took off her bangles and her rings. Then she put back her rings on her third finger, the diamond-studded wedding band and the ruby that she thought was lucky for her. For a while she flexed the finger, vigorously polishing the diamonds with her thumb. She opened her bag and put in her bangles and snapped the bag shut. For a moment I thought she was going to burst into tears.

'I know that you are going to be hurt by this and . . . and I know that you will never forgive me.'

'What's the matter?' I asked, almost in jest. 'You are not

going to leave me?'

'I think so. I've been thinking about it for a long time. But now I feel things have really reached that point. I have to do something about it.'

'Do we have to talk about this here?'

She didn't say anything. The aloo parathas, the kababs and the water without ice came. Kishen set down the plates, then the knives and forks wrapped up in paper napkins. We ate in silence and confusion. People ate and left, table by table. Kishen hovered around us, picked up the plates and brought the milky, frothy coffee.

'You may as well tell me,' I said. 'Whatever it is, it can't be too bad now.'

As I said it I was not looking at Mina. I was watching, in the gray and green veranda beyond the ledge, the intense bargaining for a pair of cushion covers.

Mina was silent, stirring her coffee.

'Is it about Rajiv?' I asked and looked at her directly.

Silence.

'Isn't it?'

A couple of people in the veranda turned at my raised voice.

'Yes.' I could almost hear a sigh of relief in her whisper.

'And of course, as we know, it isn't the first time.'

'No.'

There was nothing much else to say. We both began to sip our coffee. It was too hot; it scalded my tongue.

'You knew?' It was almost an accusation, as if I had snatched away her dream act, read it all the night before the big performance.

I nodded. My lower lip was trembling, I realized. I rested my elbow on the table and cupped my chin in my hand. Something was scalding my eyes.

Beyond the ledge the deal had been struck. The cushion covers were being packed and as soon as she got the packet the woman in the black kurta, a wooden comb stuck in her thick hair, was again opening the packet, making sure that she had been given the right pair.

Never trust anything, I thought.

Kishen had begun to hover around again, picking up the coffee cups, pocketing his tip, swishing his duster quickly over the table. The circles made by the coffee cups spread and then vanished, rubbed forever into that afternoon.

3

It was all very civilized, all very modern. We only fought once in the ten days that she stayed in the house after telling me that she was leaving. That was the night when I asked her about Ankur.

'Of course, he will go with me. What else?'

'Why will he go with you? He's my bloody son.'

'Don't curse the boy. It is not his fault.'

'I am not cursing him and it's all your fault anyway.'

'He's too young. He has to be with me. You cannot take care of him, I'm not leaving him here under any condition.'

I think I broke some things. An inkpot that made a blue-black splash on the bedroom wall near the wardrobe. A Polish crystal flower vase that I knew she particularly liked. It splintered in thick angled pieces that could cut an artery. She banged the door and left the room, screaming that I was mad and that this was no way of sorting out things. As I picked up the pieces of crystal and collected them on a newspaper, I thought for a wild moment that I would sue her in court and ask for Ankur's custody. I would prove that I could take better care of him than any mother, certainly a mother like Mina who had chosen purely for personal pleasure—or lust—to break up a family. But Mina would turn around and list out in exasperating detail, with her index finger ticking off things in the air, her brown mole twitching sexily for the judge, how she had always been the one to take care of Ankur, how she had given birth to him by having her abdomen—all three layers—cut open, how she knew exactly what he needed, how much vitamins, calcium, inoculations, coaching lessons. And what did I know about all of it anyway? I could barely remember, she would tell the world, what class he was studying in and that the only time I had gone to buy a woollen trouser for him, I had come back with a gray piece of cloth that had wash-n-wear written in large letters on the border. That was only to be expected, she would no doubt digress, from a man who had once bought expensive imported yellow squash thinking it was a rather ripe cucumber.

No; the thought of haggling over my son in a court in Patiala House, where unshaven men in handcuffs were being led through the corridors, where touts and typists hustled the crowd and lawyers in black coats stepped gingerly through puddles of rainwater, sickened me.

My son would not have to face any such thing, even though I would have to see him leave in Rajiv's shining car. It hurt me the most to see that happen. It was a bigger car than mine; it probably had a better air-conditioner and a CD player. It had been washed and polished until it shone. It was just like Rajiv to wash and polish his car for this occasion. Just to prove, as if he still needed to, that he was a better man than I, that his car, unlike mine, would not be perpetually full of old magazines, cigarette butts, peanut shells, old cash memos. Ankur sat in the back seat, helped in by Rajiv with excessive care. The kind of care that was so obviously insincere, meant to touch Mina, who was watching from the front seat, her head half turned, a blue band in her hair. I watched them from my bedroom window, from a crack between the curtains, and I remembered the day she had bought the band, from the shop in the archway that connects the front and back portions of Khan Market. That was her blue phase, everything—her kurtas, her curtains, her nail polish, her eye shadow, her shoes, her Fab India bedcovers—was in shades of blue. It made her think of the rain, the sea, the open endless skies, she said.

The same blue, not quite pale, not quite turquoise, is touching up the morning sky now, beyond the river. The river too should have been blue. But under the heavy girders of the railway bridge, I can see only gray tired water, burdened with sewage, moving helplessly down, curving in disinterested eddies and swirls. This river is blue where it is young. I have stood where it comes out of the hills and rushes past round white stones, unaware of the filth lying ahead that it is destined to carry. Everything is beautiful and innocent when it is young. I shut my eyes. I don't want to see east Delhi waking up in concrete cooperative complexes, buying milk, going to school, trudging to jobs, clinging on to crowded buses. It's an ugly sight and I hunger for beauty.

4

For several weeks after Mina left I stayed at home. Alone, except for Balram who came in every morning and evening to cook my meals and wash my clothes. Alone with the ragtag bundle of loose ends of a half-lived-out life spread out in front of me like the contents of a long-forgotten drawer suddenly emptied out on the carpet. The sunshine hurt my eyes, traffic noises grated on my nerves; the chirping of birds at dawn in the lawn behind my room broke my heart.

On the third day I tried to find my old diary and when after two hours of going through briefcases, desks and shelves I did not find it, I saw that its loss too was destined to happen and I thanked all the gods that I knew that I couldn't be tempted to call anyone, to tell my story to some half-willing but kind friend picked up at random at twilight from those fraying pages, to justify to the world what need not be justified, to provide the incestuous social circuits of Delhi with one more item of gossip. I realized then that things had reached a certain end, knew that thereafter, it could only be downhill.

I gave up the search for the diary just as I had given up Mina. Just like that, just as I accept the hills and the sunsets. It is easy, once you have taken the decision.

So I called no one and I do not remember that the telephone ever rang. Except once when Joy called after I had not turned up at the office for two days. I was not well, I told her. It was typhoid, a strange antibiotic-resistant typhoid that would take its time and while she was trying to comprehend that, I told her that I did not want anybody from the office to come and see me, that I was dangerously infectious, that they could send me flowers if they liked. I left it at that, not waiting for her to respond.

I could not make myself go into Ankur's room and see it clean and neat, all tied up with no clothes on the floor, no games scattered under the bed, no colour pens and computer games cluttering the desk. So I shut myself in my room, the one with the double bed, the television and the air-conditioner, ignoring the rest of the apartment. At one time I had plans for that apartment. I had thought that I would buy it; that I would finally convince the old landlord to sell it to me at a reasonable price. But he hadn't come back from Dubai and now, with Mina and Ankur gone, I did not care if he never did. That one room was enough for me, to live in, to sulk, to regret, to lick my wounds. If I got fed up or if the power cuts shut off the air-conditioner I could always open the double door and walk out into the little postage stamp of a lawn that I shared with my neighbour. At least now I no longer had to guard myself against Mina's nagging reproach that I could never do the right thing at the right time, that I lived in a make-believe world of my own. Unlike Rajiv, I suppose, though she never said it, who had bought property at the right time, got the house built just right, with high ceilings, real teak wood, bay windows.

On the round table in my room were three different brands of whisky, a bottle of gin, an unopened bottle of Bacardi and in the small fridge there was enough ice and mineral water for many evenings. I had Rajiv there. He couldn't drink any of this stuff without throwing up. All he could take was white wine. How could anyone get a kick out of white wine? All I had ever got was a bad headache and a sore throat in the morning.

There were three or four books by my bedside, enough cigarettes and a large ashtray. In this room I could shut myself off from all the people whom I did not want to meet; I could cut off all the sounds that I did not want to hear. Even my past rarely entered that room; it was all there in other parts of the house, packed up mostly in the cardboard cartons that Mina is supposed to come and pick up some day. It was all best kept packaged away, safe in the dark, untouched, unrecalled. The way Mina had left it, organized, catalogued in an old exercise book, noted and marked in her most matter-of-fact manner. Much of it was in that third room that we called the guest room. No guest had ever really stayed there. In truth, it was Mina's spare bedroom, the one that she used to move into whenever things got really bad between her and me. When a shutter would come down between us, a shutter of mutual recriminations, harsh words and vicious barbs. When everything about her, the way she backcombed her hair, brushed her teeth again and again, loaded her eyes with mascara even at night, would irritate me. Or I suppose when my bad breath, my habit of leaving my clothes on the ground, my desire to slurp my morning cup of tea made her want to get a break from me. Gradually, over the last few years, things that were important to her had moved there. Her shelf of books, her folders of college degrees, certificates, letters of recommendation. Most of her make-up stuff was in that room with her round mirror in which she would examine her pores closely for hours on weekends and then begin to repair the places where the years were making their first hesitant marks. Her parents' photograph and, mercifully, her precious Indian classical vocal CDs had also moved to another table in that room. That was the room into which she had moved when I discovered two years ago, though I did not confront him then, that Rajiv was not just an old friend of the family.

But this time, moving to that room had not been far enough.

I was glad she had sorted out the stuff, stuck it with duct tape and put it away. It would have all been meaningless to me and needlessly painful. Photographs, newspaper cuttings, old letters, scraps of poetry, greeting cards mean something only when they can be shared. Otherwise one is just fooling oneself and I am too old to do that any more. I preferred to leave that part of the house with its folded-up past to Balram.

Early in the morning with the sky still a dark gray, the air still damp, the night not quite gone, I would open the bedroom door and pick up the newspaper from the lawn, tossed there by the newspaper boy from his cycle basket, sometimes into a flowerpot, sometimes under the old armchair. That newspaper with its coalition politics, its murders on the third page, obituaries, lost and founds, matrimonial ads, ponderous op-ed articles, gaudy photographs of rich socialites on incongruously cheap newsprint, inedible recipes . . . that was all that I could handle of the world outside. On some days when I couldn't even handle that much, the newspaper ended up in the kitchen trashcan, half crumpled, half folded. Mina would never have allowed that. The kitchen trashcan was meant for kitchen trash; the newspapers had to be ironed out better than new and piled up in a corner of the garage, in monthly bundles tied up with string. That was part of good manners, her father had told her—evidently he had judged people all his life by how they folded the newspaper, whether the heels of their shoes were as carefully polished as their toes, how they put fork and knife together on a plate, how neat their writing tables were and such other nonsense. And then I would have breakfast, cereal and cold milk, in a deliberately chosen mug from the shelf full of mugs bought as souvenirs on holidays and weekends with Mina from some sunny Sunday market or a faraway riverside museum under a sharp blue sky full of squawking seagulls and landing planes. Yes, buying coffee mugs to remember times and places was another personal indulgence, one of the few that I had shared with Mina. I was a little surprised that she had left all of them for me and not decided to go fifty-fifty.

On most evenings I fought off the darkness in my own silly ways. I fought it by having a bath, by taking a nap, usually by pouring myself a drink. I know I liked that part, when I circled around the bottles and glasses on the round table, choosing what the drink of the day would be. Would it be a light scotch with ice and lots of tangy fresh bubbly soda? Or would it be peaty smoky single malt from the highlands or a bittersweet Bacardi and Coke? And all the time I wondered whether it was all right to go ahead and pour myself one. All I had ever heard of drinking alone stood in the way. Wasn't it supposed to be the ultimate loneliness to drink alone, a slow-motion suicide, a final decadent act of masturbation, a solitary celebration of loss and dejection? But then I would pick up a glass and let these thoughts fall away. They were only a routine act that had to be played out, a game against oneself, lost before it was begun. And when the first sip of the drink went burning down my throat, hunting out its own new path into my consciousness, I knew that I had to do it. These thoughts about drinking alone are a luxury that only people who do not have to be alone can afford. If one can sleep alone, wake up alone, eat alone, think alone, talk under one's breath day after day, why can one not drink alone? Several evenings, with such thoughts on my mind, I dozed off on my armchair on the narrow veranda opening into the lawn, a fallen magazine at my side, my third drink still unfinished.

And when I got up with too much drink in my head, my throat parched, my eyes swollen inside, I knew that I needed to get a hold on myself. Anguish, guilt, shame, holding Ankur's future in their arms, crowded around my morning mug of tea like a bunch of convinced jurors. He was only ten years old; he did not need to suffer. Or grow up with the idea that it was his father, an alcoholic manic-depressive, who had spoilt it all. Someday he would need to be told all the truths, all the stories that we hide away from children, and if I did not take care of myself there would be no one left to tell him. On some days when it became too much to take, I would cringe and shut my eyes and go back to bed and wait for everything to get better.

Often, taking a cold shower helped, at least momentarily. The water hit my face and went down my body, washing away the heavy sluggishness, erasing the forbidding faces of the jurors, and I would begin to judge myself more lightly again. After all it was I who had been wronged. I was the Victim, not the Guilty Party. I had not wronged anyone; if anything, I had played it too right. I must never let go of that basic fact. That was the only way to go on living. Good son, good student, good husband, good father. Or at least that's what I would like to think. When I could convince myself of these basic truths, I was happy. When I could not and the will to fight left me, there was no hope other than that the day would end and I would live through the evening, switching on only the most essential lights, opening only the doors that really needed to be opened, just the crack of the wardrobe, a vague peep into a drawer. On such evenings, it was especially easy to have a drink and sometimes two or three or four. I owed myself that much reprieve.

Finally, I think four or five weeks after Mina and Ankur had gone, I looked at my full beard in the bathroom mirror and I shaved. Deliberately and determinedly, like I was peeling off a layer of life, wiping it off from the bathroom sink and flushing it away with the force of flowing water. And I felt that if the phone rang now I would not be afraid to pick it up, that if I sat down to have a drink in the evening, I would be able to stop again after two whiskies. I began again to do everyday things—sending clothes for a wash, putting on the lights in the different rooms, looking into the mailbox with at least curiosity if not expectation, polishing my shoes . . . and finally, going back to the office.

5

To that wretched office in Connaught Place. I know it is called something else now but for me it will always remain Connaught Place. No matter what you call it, it is, generally speaking, a lousy place. It is one of the lousiest places in Delhi; in fact it is the lousy centre of what has become, for the most part, a lousy city.

Connaught Place has too many parked cars and too many cars on the roads. Cheap little tinny cars that will dent if you squeeze them with the hard part of your thumb. And it takes too long to get there from home. Before I, or Mina and I, got our new car—one of these Korean affairs that everyone is buying nowadays, the one that looks like a squat loaf of bread—I used to crumple up into a desperate sweaty bundle before I had cleared two red lights and reached Moolchand hospital. I hated all the people I met at the red lights every day—the woman who has aged a hundred years selling agarbattis since her husband was garlanded on a Delhi street with a burning tyre in 1984, the man with a sewn stump for an arm selling facial tissues, the boys with infected watering eyes selling colourful calculators, and on Saturdays, everybody with little pans of oil, tin shani devtas floating in them, begging you to pay up or threatening you with an eternal curse.

Who cared about those curses any longer? There was, a short drive from where I cowered, a more able man than I who had claimed my wife and child. The world was already doing its worst. Things could only get better.

Things are supposed to get better at those red lights when the flyovers are finally built. I have seen in these last few months the huge pillars coming up everywhere; strangely, however, there is no sound. I remember that when they built the first flyover in

Delhi, the one near Defence Colony, the piledrivers made deafening thuds for months. It seemed that the old roads of Delhi were being pounded into dust with each massive drive, the past was being thrust into the remains of the seven cities already buried deep and a new future with swinging, sweeping flyovers complete with bright mercury lights and ice cream vans was being built to solve all our problems. A senseless world of speed and certitude.

Every time I go over that old flyover I can still feel the faraway echo of that piledriver in my bones. I can feel the yellow heat of that long-gone summer with its searing winds. It was in that summer that we gathered in curtained rooms waiting for the evening and the magic hour of orange bar ice creams, glasses of chilled sweet lemonade and the welcome scent of wet earth as the gardener sprinkled water on the parched flower beds. That summer, along with the relentless thudding of the piledrivers we heard the tortured coughing of my mother's grandmother, the ancient, quiet lady who used to hide dry fruits for me from the rest of the world. That summer she began to die.

Cursing the place under my breath, I finally found parking on Barakhamba road. The boy who took my key and gave me a thin yellow unreadable counterfoil looked at me with undisguised scorn. I had been away too long, his look seemed to say. Four or five weeks is a long time and parking spots in Connaught place do not wait for people who choose to be away so long. Typhoid, I wanted to tell him but knew that he would not have believed it. The world moves, life continues, his look would have said. I would have to take what I could get and slowly, if I was nice and regular, I would build up my credit with him again until it was strong enough for him to smile at me, take my key and cockily reverse the car into a convenient spot shaded by a tree.

I pushed myself through the crowd, trying to walk so that my white shirt did not touch too many shoulders. There was a time when I could saunter through Connaught Place. People came there for a stroll in the evenings, couples came to hold sweaty, nervous hands near the fountain, to eat paan or homemade mango ice cream in green leaves, or have elegant tea with cheese balls in restaurants that smelt of ice cream wafers, listening to juke-boxed music playing fifties' tunes. Now I had to manoeuvre my way through an army of handkerchief sellers, key-chain sellers, banana sellers, past charpoys of fake leather wallets, three-in-one-packet underwear, calendars, diaries, and chaatwalas with boiled potatoes and unpeeled kachalus and tomatoes and lemons already set up at nine in the morning. Some people eat chaat for breakfast!

I wished I didn't have to do this; I wished the office was in some other place. Perhaps on the first floor of a house on a leafy, quiet street in Jorbagh or Golf Links or in the new Habitat Centre. I would be able to work so much better in those places. But the company had bought space in that building at a time when it made sense to buy that place, a time when white shirts stayed white through the day. And nobody gives up space once bought in Connaught Place, not even the boot polish boy outside the new Statesman House or the one-eyed man selling ballpoint pens and refills near the American Library. Then, the building used to be a new, shiny place with a famous boutique already set up on the ground floor and a stylish restaurant on the mezzanine floor, the sort of place where business executives came for lunches for two. The boutique didn't last two months, the restaurant is now the office of a travel agency.

I was not alone in that building, just one among several thousand. But I was one of the few who remembered the building from the early days. All glass and marble, stone murals in brown and ochre on the walls, fire extinguishers with typed instructions in the staircases, glasses in the metal-framed windows. And I remembered Panditji as a young man, proud of his lift, all steel and mirrors and with a spittoon and a little metal notice saying that it could take only nine persons or 650 kilograms, whichever was less. Panditji is still there, sitting on his little wooden stool in the corner of the lift. He has grown old asking me about the heat outside, the rising prices, my health and my views on the Government of the day. He has grown old taking people up and down, talking and yawning. He has seen the mirrors of his lift tarnish and in these tarnished mirrors he has seen his moustache become a sagging white caricature of the once shiny black handlebar.

I don't much look into mirrors nowadays, not when I can help it, and I would avoid even the tarnished ones in Panditji's lift. I look only at parts of a mirror. I look at the point that shows where the razor is shearing the hair of my beard, I look at the place where the toothbrush is going round and round in oblong motions, clearing out the food stuck at the top edges of my teeth, I look at my red comb moving hastily through my thinning hair. But I do not look at it whole, the way I used to do when I was at college, again and again, to see how good, how smart, how absolutely heartbreaking I looked. In those fresh winters I took a long time getting out of the bath. The steam from the hot water taken from the huge drum standing on a wooden fire clouded up the small mirror in the bathroom. As I dried myself with the white-and-blue towel, across my shoulders, across my chest, under my raised strong arms, I always wanted to see myself in the mirror. With a smile of indulgent self-pride I would wipe the mirror and admire myself as I cleaned up for the world, for the future, for these damned middle-aged days. Now I hate the sight of full-length mirrors, the kind that have been put up in fancy places, in the lifts of five-star hotels, in rich rooms, in clubs, bars, shopping malls. They make me see myself whole, a stranger gone further in years than I can imagine; a tired man who seems to have missed the last bus to somewhere.

I wonder if Panditji remembers what I looked like in the old days, if he noted the change in my hair, my belly, my walk, my skin. And if he cared.

'Arre, Aftab babu, long time. What happened? Been out, foreign?'

'No, no, just like that.'

'Just like that?' He didn't believe me. 'All well I hope, no fever or flu?'

For a moment I wanted to stop the lift between floors and tell him all that had happened to me, tell him that for starters my wife had walked out on me, taking away my only son.

'No, Panditji, I am fine.'

I couldn't give him that typhoid stuff; we went back a long time.

'If you say so. But be careful. This year the heat will come very early. It is the new century, the new millennium. Kalyug. Things are changing all over the world. It's all these nuclear tests and all this construction. They have not left a single tree. You remember the shade we used to have in these parts? Bungalows and trees. Bungalows made by Englishmen, trees planted by Englishmen. They went away and all that they built has also gone after them.'

The lift jerked to a halt on the eighth floor, the doors creaked open and I walked out, my eyes fixed on my shoes. I left Panditji on his stool, a wrinkled hand on one aching knee, the other twirling the end of his moustache, to ruminate for yet another day, over a lost world.

My office room looked like someone had packed it all up as if I would never come back, almost as if I had died and they were now waiting for someone, some next of kin, to come and pick up the mementoes and make place for the next Manager of Public Relations, some guy with gelled black hair, a six pack under a classy white shirt, a foreign degree, a slippery American accent. Perhaps that had been Basu's wishful thinking and he had given instructions for the clean up. I felt anger rising to my head and fought down the urge to stride into his room, interrupt his morning breakfast of idli and sambar and let him have it. I have never understood why he doesn't have breakfast at home before coming to office. It's not as if he isn't hungry. The first thing he does as soon as he enters his room, winter or summer, is step on his buzzer and ask for his beloved idli, as if he hasn't eaten anything for days. Perhaps in some mean, complicated, calculating way of his, this is all part of a far-sighted saving plan that will make all the difference between him and me when we retire. It might enable him to play golf, or buy a better last car, or even, in the end, die in a cleaner hospital.

My table was clean, there were no newspapers or magazines lying around, the wastepaper basket was empty. Dust covers had been put on my computer and printer. All that was needed was a wreath of chrysanthemums and a Rest in Peace sign on the desk. I looked around for my plants. Even those had been moved, but fortunately only to Joy's room; I could see them through the glass separation. I began to cool down. Probably she had put them there so she could water them regularly; probably it was she who had made sure that my room was kept clean and tidy.

It was obvious that those weeks of my absence had not been

a total loss for Joy. She had taken it easy with nothing to do except do herself up, work out a new image. She's always doing something of the sort. She is an avid reader of a column that comes in one of the dailies, I forget which one—they all seem the same with their smudged colour photographs on bad newsprint. That's the five-ways column—you know the kind of stuff—five ways to colour your hair, five ways to organize your room, five ways to have a great body, five ways to paint your wretched nails. I wonder if they will ever come out with five ways to fuck. I'll keep a cutting of that column under the glass top of my table, I promise, just like Joy keeps all her favourites.

She had obviously read some good stuff in those weeks that I had been at home. She had lost weight and looked fit enough to pass for thirty, though I knew from her file that she would be forty-two next October. Nobody could guess that unless of course they had access to that personal file or they looked at her long enough to notice the way her skin hung in rings around her collarbone and wrinkled up in concentric circles around her elbows. That's where most women show their age—some days, even on the streets, walking, I find myself staring at women's arms, counting the circles of wrinkles like one counts the circles on the stump of an old tree.

I noticed that Joy had done something to her hair; they looked freshly washed, and not even quite dry or properly combed. Her role model seemed to have changed in those weeks, from the spick and span, efficient and not unattractive secretary to some sultry seductress with heavy lidded eyes and not quite dry, open long hair. I thought that one day I would have to tell her, in my most officious bossy voice: Look here, Joy, this is an office, you know, not some fancy farmhouse party. I'd like you to comb and dry your hair before you come to office or I will have to grab a comb and do it myself . . . But then that would have amounted to sexual harassment, exactly what Basu would have wanted. Besides, somebody else had no doubt told her in the first place that this hair suited her immensely, brought out her true inner personality, or some such trash. Perhaps, I felt with a surprising twinge of betrayal, it was Basu who had complimented her on her new hairstyle during my absence, walking past her desk, one hand thrust deep into his trouser pocket, the second fingering the star of his Mont Blanc.

So I decided against saying anything. It wouldn't have made any difference and it might just have put her off for a couple of days and she would have sulked and stopped making my coffee. Instead I smiled sweetly and told her I was much better except for some residual weakness in my legs which stays for weeks after typhoid and yes, I was taking care of myself and drinking only orange juice morning and night and could she please sometime later, no hurry just yet, bring my plants back to my room so that I could feel among the living again. Then, after I had sipped my coffee and felt the strength surge through my nerves, I told her to start putting all those wretched names, telephone numbers and addresses that I had lost, the strands of my splintered life, the miserable remnants of all those years of giving and giving, together again.

She didn't do too badly for that first day. She put together three pages with names, addresses and telephones, all sorted out alphabetically on her computer. No doubt she expected that—the alphabetical part—to impress me. I have never told her that I went through all this computer stuff three years ago, much before she started taking evening classes in word processing. I suppose she took those classes to improve her prospects, move on to a better job, to climb up the ladder. Maybe she would and maybe she wouldn't. Somewhere along the line poor Joy, my poor old once-upon-a-time sexy Joy, my curious, tatty and middle-class Joy would realize that ladders don't matter. They don't lead anywhere; the more you climb the more you have to climb. All you need to do is to find a step on that ladder where it is wide and comfortable and there's no fear of falling off and then the trick is to stay there. Because there is no step from which you can't be pushed off. I wanted to catch hold of her and tell her, 'I'm holding on to my step, Joy, and I know old Basu is trying to push me off. And I also know that in the end I don't have the staying power. I can already feel the weakness in my wrists and in my forearms. One day he'll push me off, but I'll give him a fight yet.' I wanted to tell her of the great clarity that descended on my mind all those nights when I could not sleep and lit it up like a carnival from the inside. I would pace the small lawn restlessly and watch the occasional three-wheeler or drunk labourer going home and would finally pour myself another whisky, three fingers deep, and put in my three cubes of ice, and feel that I could still give it all a damn good go. If only I could pull myself together and if only I could convince myself that the fight would be worth it in the end.

She left those three pages unobtrusively on my table. I wondered how she had managed to do it so fast, something that I had built up painstakingly over many years, block by block, in black, green, blue ink. It must have been all that listening in to my conversations, I suppose. Or perhaps she just had a natural talent that had made her a secretary in the first place, an ability to listen, note, file and recall. Perhaps she had little scribble pads with Charlie Brown smile covers in which she had scribbled in every random name, telephone number and address that she had found on my table or in the visiting cards that I had thrown away.

However she did it, at the end of the day I had three pages of my diary back and I could have bet that she had kept a copy, just in case I lost them all over again or perhaps just out of curiosity or, more likely, to add a certain touch of reality to her lunchtime gossip.

If I wanted then, I could have sat in my office and called each of the names on those three pages and asked them what they planned to do that evening or the next day or over the weekend or during the summer holidays. I could have told them cheerily that Mina was gone and I was again a free man and I could have begun to meet them all again, become a part of birthdays, anniversaries, promotion parties, end- or beginning-of-season parties, just parties. Carefully planned parties, each with its tailored, thought-out guest list, its ostensible purpose and its hidden purpose, its menus and agendas and cocktails and in the end with its clutter, its ashtrays full of burnt-out cigarettes, memories of intense or desultory conversations, barbs, hints, innuendoes, visiting cards. But the very thought sickened me and I recoiled from it with an almost physical horror. I folded away those three pages and put them into the left-hand side drawer of my table, the one in which I kept the restaurant guide and postage stamps and my guilt-box with Rohini's last letter and our only photograph together.

Let Joy complete the rest of the numbers, if she can, I thought, and until then I could wait. After all *I* lost my diary, all of them hadn't lost theirs.

And yet the phone had not rung at home for many days.

When finally it did one night in early December, I let it go on and on, watching the instrument intensely as if to identify the caller from the sound, to judge his or her sincerity by its shrill tone. Did the ring have Mina's insistence in it? Was it someone who really wanted to talk to me or simply wanted me to do something for him? Was it someone who had felt obliged to make that phone call or someone who really wanted to talk to me, me as against the whole wide world? The ringing stopped and I thought that I would never know the answers to my neurotic questions. Then it rang again and almost immediately I picked it up.

6

It was Jamshed. And that meant it was also his wife Brinda and their twenty-one-year-old buck-toothed daughter Rohan and their fat, hamburger-and-potato-chips-infested son. I always forget his name. I've always forgotten his name since he was born, all those years ago, in a south Delhi clinic and I and Mina, newly married, had gone there to see Brinda, carrying with us a big baby book and a baby feeding bottle as a present. I feel guilty when I look at him. Perhaps if we had not gifted that baby bottle, he may not have grown into such a monstrosity, a huge blob of junk food, holding an extra large paper glass of Coke perpetually in his hand.

Jamshed immediately went into the attack.

'Just where have you been? No call, no nothing.'

'You didn't call either.'

'Oh, I see. Now it is going to be this. I see. We didn't call. All these years and now you are standing on these formalities.'

'It's all right, Jamshed. I am fine and glad you called.'

He cooled down.

'Listen Aftab, we didn't want to seem like meddling. We knew you were sorting out things. We thought we would give you time, space but believe me, Brinda and I have been thinking of you, of Mina and you, every day. Sad, all this is very sad. Breaks my heart.'

'How is the family?'

'Rohan is exhibiting next Thursday. Triveni basement, and she is absolutely keen that you are there. You must come and also tell as many people as you can. She is depending on you a lot and all your contacts to get a big boost.'

Of course. That was why he had called, why he had always wanted me to come to all his exhibitions, to all of Brinda's exhibitions and, since the last year or so, to all of Rohan's exhibitions. I listened as he told me to ring up photographers, designers, creative editors, copywriters, models, filmmakers to come and see and admire and perhaps even buy Rohan's photographs of broken vases, coloured bracelets, piles of Holi colours, three tomatoes and a half-peeled orange, antique lamps in a shop. I could imagine them even as we spoke. And they would all no doubt be arranged in four seasons—Summer, Autumn . . . The mere thought tired me.

And they would all be Highly Overpriced. But that's the way Jamshed and Brinda have always been and still are and probably will remain to the end of their artistic days. He always overprices his sketches and she always overprices her wood sculptures. I suppose it's a marketing strategy. I think I know where it all probably began, in the poor early days when Jamshed used to paint in a barsati in Defence Colony. That one room was his studio and bedroom and salon. There were canvases, and brushes in cups, and old pieces of cloth with paint, and bare walls. His one luxury those days was plants, large leafy plants on the airy terrace that came with that one room. And Brinda, third-year psychology student at Lady Shri Ram College, fuzzy ideas about sculpture floating in her head, her grandmother's gold nose pin marking her face with an attractive distinction, would reach that barsati in the afternoons. Her first sculpture was made to stand among those green plants and the whole picture was suddenly complete. When I went to the barsati one evening, I found an empty bottle of wine and two glasses near her sandals at the edge of the mattress on the floor and the smell of love-making mingled with the sharpness of oil paints. I envied them that afternoon; I envied them their courage and freedom, their artistic natures and their runaway love.

That was probably when they decided to be rich one day. There is some sense to their strategy, I suppose. Whoever is fool enough to buy one of their pieces would have spent so much money that he would rather put up the piece in his drawing room and not in the study or the corridor or the bedroom. It will be put where people can see it or talk about it or walk up to peer at it closely and perhaps even ask, in a blushing display of impolite manners, how much the wretched thing cost. That would of course be just what the host would be waiting for—and, somewhere in his studio faraway, also Jamshed, paint brush in one hand, the other distractedly combing his free-growing beard. An expensive sketch has a way of acquiring the grace of a Picasso, and one day it is likely to be sought after and perhaps even be put up for an auction. I always thought Brinda the more sensible of the two with her feet solidly on the ground in the manner of her heavy wooden sculptures. She tried, I think, early on in their careers, to make him cut down the prices and sell more—build up brand equity as they say. Let more of the sculptures and sketches be put up in more corridors so that people, many people, see them while they take off their coats and shawls and while they glance discreetly at mirrors. Let them become so well known that people cast just a glance at a canvas of fading browns and whisper, artfully, between sips of wine, Oh, that's a Jamshed, or at a vision of smooth wooden curves and exclaim—Oh, when did you get that Brinda piece? But Brinda's sensible strategy never took off; Jamshed quickly overruled her.

In any case, I don't know why it used to bother me so much. I could always go to their exhibitions and not buy anything. I could for instance have gone that time to Rohan's photographic exhibition, just walked around, looked intelligently at the photographs, made some rather obvious and obtuse comments about light and angles, shook hands with the many mutual friends who would no doubt have been there, stayed for a glass of wine and then simply walked away. I mean, *technically* speaking, there was nothing to stop me from doing that. After all, Jamshed had merely wanted me to come just for the sake of coming, just for the benefit of my comments on the work of an up-and-coming young photographer, just for giving the event the right amount of gravitas, experience, dignity and respect.

But then, when was the last time I walked off from an exhibition, by any member of the family, without buying at least one thing? Perhaps because I have always felt that somehow it would not be correct to just walk out, that it would *look bad*, that Jamshed or Brinda would think that I didn't like their work enough, that I didn't like *them* enough, that I was some sort of traitor to the pact made in that Defence Colony barsati.

I don't even know where all the stuff has gone, perhaps Mina knows. She always liked Jamshed's sketches, since the day he did a quick drawing of her sitting on the edge of a sofa next to a leather lamp in the early months of our marriage. The leather lamp has a large hole in the shade now and Mina is gone but that sketch was still on the dining-room wall when I shut up the house. I think she deliberately left it there, to torture me in some way. A simple line sketch, rather well done. The resemblance is complete, the drawing fluid. Jamshed had something passionate and genuine in him, at least then. He never made a sketch of Mina and me together though he kept talking about it all the time. So maybe it's right that she should know where all the stuff of his that I bought is kept, in which suitcase, cupboard or garage.

Some of the sketches I think were even lying in the office, packed in bubble paper. They must have all been pinched by Basu now and maybe passed on to his beloved Neeta. I should have called up Mina and told her to take them all away before I left the office. I could have given some of them away to Joy as farewell gifts. She'd have been greatly tickled and might even have thought that I was making a sort of final artistic pass at her. *That* would have tickled her. She is just the kind that likes artistic courting with poetry and paintings and little snippets in senseless blank verse. I could have then told her that I wanted to go to bed with her, that I had wanted to go to bed with her since the day she had walked into the office. I would have liked to see if *that* tickled her.

7

This train has all the disadvantages of an airplane without any of the advantages. The seats are narrow and three on each side of the aisle. I am crushed against the window and unlike in an airplane, there is no red wine to help me through it all. A man in a black uniform that I cannot recognize is sitting next to me. He has very white teeth under a heavily dyed bristling moustache and I can smell the brilliantine in his hair. I know he is dying to talk to me, to pass the time, as he would no doubt say. As if that is all that

I am left good for now, to help some joker in a fraud uniform pass the time on the way to his home town. If he does start to talk, I will tell him that I usually charge for this privilege. For the last twenty minutes I have been putting off the urge to go to the toilet. I will have to go past him and to do that I will have to ask him to fold his meal tray that he has had open since the train set off. And if I talk to him I will set off the dreaded conversation.

So I shut my eyes and pretend to be asleep, letting my mind jog to the sound, however muffled, of the rolling wheels.

Those days it was a thirty-two-hour journey from Delhi to Bombay. There was excitement in the night, music in the air and girls in the next compartment as we headed out to a college cultural festival. The train wound its way leisurely towards Bombay over long bridges that spanned yawning stony beds, through silent trees and across little deserted road crossings with their one lonely red light and kerosene lantern. It stopped often, giving way across the dark plain to faster trains, waiting outside the big junctions till it got a berth. That's how it took thirty-two hours. At one such stop I pulled on my canvas shoes and airman jacket with the fur collar and went to the end of the corridor. Everybody seemed to be asleep except for the conductor and another man, both smoking beedis at the door, collars turned up against the cold. A small boy in a rough, loosely knit monkey cap that covered his head and neck leaving only a little window for his face was pouring tea from an aluminum kettle into brown earthen cups. The tea tasted of baked mud but it was hot and sweet. The moon threw a ghostly light across the plain; the stars seemed nearer than ever before.

A red light far along the tracks marked the entry to some big junction. Beyond it the lights of the town rose in a faraway glow into the sky. I walked along the train. I felt free and fresh. There was so much to the world, to life, to the future, to the present. I glanced up, feeling instinctively that somebody was looking at me. It was one of the girls from the other compartment, going to the same festival in Bombay, looking through the glass, sleepy eyed. And so pale that she shone in the moonlight. Without thinking I raised the earthen cup of tea towards her. She smiled, a lazy sleepy smile, and nodded slightly. I hurried to the boy near the door, hoping that the train would not begin to move. Miraculously the train stood still while I bought the tea and handed her the cup. Her thin white hand came through the half raised window and hurriedly went back, as if frightened at the touch of the cold air. She cupped the tea in both hands and the steam slowly clouded up the window until I could barely see her. Then the train lurched and I threw my cup into the thorny bushes below the rail lines and rushed back to my berth.

The train loitered through the brown plain of central India. It took long detours as if deliberately holding back from its destination, playing a game of snakes and ladders through the land of the red soil, the black soil and the rocky ravines with their empty echoing riverbeds and legends of dacoits. We sat on the steps and held the cold steel rails and let the country flow through our minds along with the winds that knew no end. We saw the evening fall on the hundreds of villages where the cow dung burnt and sent its wintry smoke up into the huge overturned bowl of the sky. In the morning we sat in the old-world dining car with tables and folded white napkins, salt and pepper dispensers, pewter ashtrays, a single paper flower on each table. I have looked for that dining car across continents but found only hurried meals, sandwiches, coffee in takeaway cups in neat, efficient places, never the languid leisure of the two tables across which introductions and conversational gambits had been exchanged over coffee and undersalted omelettes.

Six days later, after the heady rush of the festival, that pale beauty became the first girl that I kissed. The cutting edge of her perfume as I nestled my face in her hair and the vision of the huge belly of a plane as I glanced over her shoulder, its red and green lights twinkling as it went over the sea, remained with me for a long time. I still have the halting note with which she said goodbye, lying folded somewhere in an old wallet that has long lost its shape.

I think it is that memory that makes train journeys so nostalgic for me. Air journeys only make me horny. I suppose it is something to do with all the wine or the height or the airhostesses. The silken swish of their sarees as they walk past, brushing their sides against my shoulder, the stretch of their skirts across their backs, or simply the knowledge that all those women are confined along with me in a narrow enclosed space. Then I play out all the sex I can inside my head. That was one of the things that irritated Mina, one of the things, I'm sure, that ultimately made her walk out on me. She wanted more of the real thing, in bed, hour after bloody hour, and I was never quite up to that.

8

After she left, Mina called me up once in a while and unconsciously, through my confusion and my hate, I waited for her phone call. I have always waited for her phone calls through the last fourteen years while I secretly prayed that it should be she who should be waiting for me to call and that I would have the strength, that I would be man enough to make her wait. But I couldn't do it at twenty-six and I couldn't do it at forty. What's more, at forty I didn't even feel like pretending. I did not think that I had the time to pretend any more. So I waited for her calls and I am even waiting now, dreading the phone on this moving train. I know she cannot do it; she won't do it on this journey unless I tell her where I am. This is not the sort of train that has telephones on it and I returned my cellphone the day I left office, feeling free and unchained. Some of that sense of freedom has persisted. I feel I can, one day, start afresh. Once I am over the loneliness, the depression, the indulgent self-pity part of it, maybe I can begin to even enjoy my single status. Do all the things I couldn't do because it meant multiplying the cost of everything by three. Perhaps someday I can take a cruise or a flight to Iceland or trek to Kailash Mansarovar or wander along the charmed cities of the silk route. Or even do the unthinkable, go to some strange city and coolly walk into a singles bar . . . No, that begins to sound seedy again.

Sometimes Mina called me at work. Those were the most difficult, the office calls. I could almost see the hidden smile on Joy's face as she buzzed me and at the same time leaned closer to the glass partition to make sure, as it were, that I had heard the buzzer and picked up the phone. I couldn't help feeling that she was listening in and even if she was not, merely looking at me through the glass partition was enough to allow her to hear all that Mina was saying to me. I didn't care much if she heard what I was saying. It was usually yes or no or let's see or I think so or I'll try my bloody best. Non-committal, non-revealing, almost non-meaning, if you know what I mean. But I didn't want Joy, or for that matter anyone, to know what Mina was telling me. I didn't want them to know that she was still playing with every aspect of my life, that she was still virtually opening my cupboard and looking around for her scarf among my underwear or rifling through my most precious twenty-year-old scraps of paper while looking for an airmail envelope or that she was still keeping me chained and plastered and stretched out with her network of innocent questions and remarks. Obliged to her, when I come to think of it, for nothing at all—just the way she wanted it.

But most of the time she talked about herself. The last time she rang up she talked about the woman who is running the child relief agency for which Mina has started doing some art designs. They would use them for greeting cards and calendars and stuff like that. The stupid lady, the boss that is, would be better off running a travel bureau or a hairdressing salon or a cookery class. She, according to Mina, had no clue about children, no feel for relief work or art. What is more, she had no Sympathy, and you cannot run relief agencies for orphaned children, delinquent children unless you have Sympathy dripping from every pore of your being. I listened to her for twenty-five minutes and kept wondering why I didn't just put the phone down. I didn't owe her this any more, I didn't owe her anything. I didn't owe anything to anybody.

She—they all—owed me one hell of a lot.

But I listened and all the time I watched Joy through the glass window, putting on a fresh coat of crimson lipstick just before leaving office for lunch. I used to often wonder where she went for lunch. Did she eat every day in the staff dining room or did she step out into the crowded heat of Connaught Place? If it had been Bombay, at least the Bombay that I knew all too briefly, I suppose she would have gone to any of those secretary-laden sandwich-and-salad joints around Flora Fountain where she would have mingled easily with her type, thin-legged women in A-line dresses full of gossip about their middle-aged bosses, and there she would have thrilled all the others with stories of how my wife had walked out with another younger, sexier man but still called me and bulldozed me and how I still took it. They would have all gone into hysterics over the cucumber and tomato.

I found it easier to handle these phone calls at home. I had an answering machine and I didn't have Joy. I could choose when to take the call and when to pretend that I was not home and listen to her leaving a message: It's me, Mina. Call me. I need to talk to you.

Yes, and what about all the times in the last fourteen years when *I* needed to talk to her, when *I* needed her to sit down with me and listen to all my problems and my hassles. She went into her selfish shell then. The dog days of silence became the dog years of silence. And the silence began to eat into our togetherness, destroying it from the inside, like the sugar that according to Dr Rao is even now coursing at dangerously high levels through the highways and byways of my body. Silence can destroy anything; it lets the mind wander too much. It loosens the web that everyday conversation, ordinary conversation about groceries and movies and books and newspapers can weave, unobtrusively. Instead of telling me what was going wrong with us, she chose to be silent. Instead of listening to my dark doubts, she pushed me into sullen silence. Why call me now?

I usually took the call when she said that it was about Ankur. She knew that I would take all those calls but she also knew that she could not use this trick too often. Otherwise, I would overcome that too and then I would not be there any more when she really needed to talk to me.

But I found it easier to talk to Mina, if I must, than meet her.

That put the fear of God in me. The first time I actually saw her after she had left was at the Gymkhana club. She was with Naini. I stood still behind one of the pillars so that they didn't see me as they came out of the small bar, deep in conversation. I wondered if the Bloody Marys and seekh kababs were still going on my account. I would need to check the bill carefully at the end of the month. On second thoughts, who cared? I would never raise it with Mina anyway. Let them have their Bloody Marys with a thick layer of salt on the glass rim, the way they liked it, and let them discuss how Rajiv is a better, more considerate, more accomplished lover than me. How he always waits for Mina, how he understands her every mood, the directions of her desire, knows exactly where to touch, when to caress, when to bite.

She has always spent a lot of time with Naini. They shared a lot of things—medium height, dark eyes, three years of fun in college, memories of first boyfriends. Now of course they share one more thing. Both of them have dumped their husbands. Mina has Rajiv and I wonder if Naini too has a lover. She looks like a woman who couldn't probably do too long without one. At times I have seen the fire in her eyes, a gleam that made me want to push her next to a corner behind a door, down on the bed, up on the dining table. That besides, I never really liked her. I put up with her because of Mina though at times that dog of hers, her beloved Chihuahua called Bonny, gave me the creeps. I have a feeling that it was that tiny freak of a dog that finally made Prashant pack up his bags and sign the papers.

She has Bonny with her all the time, in sweater pockets, peeping out of tennis bags, perched on her shoulder, an apparition in black and tan. There is a corner in her drawing room devoted to books on Chihuahuas—feeding habits, training tips, history and cultural importance, how a Mexican puppy became an

American icon. One day when I had gone to pick up Mina from her house, I went through that shelf. The most intriguing title I found was *Mother Knows Best: What Not To Do With Your Dog*. It was generously underlined; she probably read it every day. And above the bookshelf was a computer-generated banner that said: Here Dog is Family. Chastised, I moved away from the shelf.

I knew things were probably going too far when I heard her telling Mina once, 'You know, nearly 85 per cent of dogs have dental health problems; the thing is to take preventive care.' Even Mina found that a bit too much and when her surprise superseded her loyalty she told me that Naini subscribed to an American magazine on Chihuahuas and using that magazine she had ordered all sorts of stuff for Bonny's teeth—dental dinosaurs, plaque attackers, nylofloss—and Prashant had blown a fuse when he found out. Now I suppose with Prashant out of the way, she and Bonny could floss together and prevent tooth decay.

Somehow I feel that it was Naini who inspired Mina to finally pack up and leave. Without her, even with Rajiv begging, she may not have actually done it. I can't say why I have this feeling. But I do—and I have no one but myself to convince.

When I saw them walk past me in the club I felt all wrong and incompetent and useless. The same bilious feeling rose up to my throat when Mina walked into Brinda's Christmas eve party, a party with hot wine and punch that Brinda organizes every year so that she and Jamshed can be free on New Year's eve to go party hopping from the Golf club to some roomy house in Vasant Vihar and then to some fog-bound farmhouse beyond Qutub Minar with its dogs and guards.

Jamshed had insisted that I come. I suppose it had troubled him that I had actually walked off from the Triveni basement after buying just one small photograph, the nearest that I could come to buying nothing. Probably, in his own complicated way, he must have thought that I was angry about something, or out of sorts because of Mina.

'You must come. It will be good for you and it will be nice for everybody there,' he had said.

'Everybody?' I asked, my suspicions aroused.

'Oh, I don't know. You know it's always Brinda who draws up these lists. I just can't focus on all these things. I can either paint or draw up invitation lists and I would rather paint. Anyhow, just come. Christmas comes once a year, you know.'

I suppose I was tired of being alone. The house had begun to get to me, the roof seemed too low, the windows too small, the walls seemed to be moving in all the time. I thought getting out might do the trick. I did not count going to office as getting out—that was just another prison with Joy, Basu, Panditji, appointments, reputation, monthly salary . . . all sentinels with bronzed muscles standing guard. So, somewhat to Jamshed's surprise, I reached the party.

The house was lit up. Valets, looking incongruous in buttoned-up black coats and sneakers came to the porch and took the cars away to park them in line, in neutral gear so that nobody would be blocked up when the time came to leave. A large crowd had already gathered in the drawing room and spilled over to the sunken television room where a huge man in a white jacket and large black bow tie was serving drinks from behind a marble counter. From somewhere outside, perhaps from the garage or the terrace or some tent pitched in the back lawn by the caterers, roasted tikkas and kababs were carried in on plates with mint chutney and little toothpicks whose top ends were wrapped in green, red and blue cellophane paper, the kind of paper that I had used in class four in school to cover my wildlife scrapbook.

I reached the bar without being accosted by anybody I knew—it was one of those parties. The man behind the bar raised a quizzical eyebrow and managed to appear polite only by bending slightly towards me.

'Whisky, please, on the rocks.'

He felt no further need to bend and looked up directly at me.

'I only have cocktails here, sir.'

'I see. What can you make?'

All of a sudden, I wanted to pick a fight.

'Flipping Duck, Leap Frog, Chocolate Monkey, Green Eyes.'

'Green Eyes—that's new. And Chocolate Monkey—is that your own invention?'

He glared back and just then, Jamshed saw me.

'Aftab, come, come, leave all these fancy cocktails. Let me take you to the real bar.'

He led me to the study and opened a small closet. I knew that was where he kept his special whiskies, all the single malts.

'Today is special, I have to give you a special drink.'

Lovingly he fondled a new bottle.

'This, my friend, is the Rolls Royce of single malts. Macallan 1946.'

He poured half an inch each in two glasses and handed me one.

'Just smell it. Smell the heather of the north.'

'Where did you get it?'

'For a painting, my friend. One painting, one bottle. I am told only three thousand bottles came to India—each one is selling for two thousand dollars.'

I felt a deep guilt. I was used to drinking rough rum from the hills mixed with coke with Jamshed when we were young. I started calculating what that half inch must be worth.

Jamshed's eyes were shut in ecstasy. I raised my glass and wondered why I was celebrating my complete failure, my deepest losses in this most expensive way.

I talked to a lot of people that evening and I must have been rather funny and charming, judging by the number of visiting cards that I later found in my pocket. I spent a fair amount of time with a TV newsreader who was dressed like she was going to get married in a few minutes, in a violet lehnga with glittering sequins and a wide gold choker around her neck and huge bands of gold earrings. She stood there in the corner, a Green Eyes cocktail in her hand, waiting for people to troop past and pay homage. I left her when I noticed the sad lines forming at the corners of her eyes, creasing her make-up.

It was a bigger party than Brinda's usual Christmas do. Not just the artists, but also fashion designers, lawyers and doctors. The doctors intrigued me; they normally did not have a place in such parties. But these were not the old CGHS-type doctors, not the children of old Dr Rao who would have blown a scornful puff of his Red & White cigarette at the mere mention of a party. These were the new doctors, the true representatives of corporate medicine, the champions of the theory that new hearts, new arteries, new kidneys should be given to those who can buy them like new cars or refrigerators or air-conditioners. They had driven up to that party, like they drove up to other parties almost every night, in new cars given to them as bonus payments for having ordered the largest number of bypass operations or the most echocardiograms or the most angiographies or whatever. These were tough men who could drink till late at night and go to cure sick hearts in the morning, clever men armed with a great skill for almost nothing by a country that had idealistically hoped that one day they would turn around and help her solve her problems.

There was even a doctor who everybody thought was actually a spy for some foreign agency. Nobody quite knew where he worked, and yet he had suddenly acquired a new car and a farmhouse and went for holidays to fancy spots in Europe every year.

And there were women with large bindis, backless blouses, crushed cotton sarees, huge gray buns on their heads held together by large combs and needles, women in crisp silks, and hand-woven kurtas, with thick black lines to highlight their eyes, raw leather purses, raw leather chappals, and henna in their hair . . . They all belonged to the tribe that Mina had joined. I could recognize some of them, from chance encounters at the India International Centre or at Triveni. And of course I recognized the author of Joy's favourite five-ways to everything column.

I saw Mina and Rajiv enter the room before they saw me. I saw her take off her expensive cream shawl and fold it in that way she has, deliberate, thinking of something else, over her forearm. She was looking good and relaxed and happy. That was what hurt the most: happy. She was looking like she used to look in the old days, just after we had made love and she had taken a nap and a shower. I wondered if that was how she and Rajiv had spent the afternoon, enjoying each others' bodies, flaunting their new-found, unashamed togetherness.

She had a new hairdo, short and snappy, and she had done something to her eyes, something to make them seem darker all over, contrasting deeply with her fair skin. And she was in one of the outfits that she had taken to wearing during the last few months that we were together, a combination of raw silk and handmade cottons in brown and rust and dark green. She was a woman of the earth now who could not be seen in jeans and trousers or traditional colourful silks. I suppose these clothes were the uniform of her tribe, of women who work for child relief agencies, or serious magazines or non-governmental organizations. These clothes were the female equivalent of a raw silk kurta-pyjama and woollen bundi and sandals that Jamshed and the other men were wearing that evening. Rajiv was wearing one of those sets too, a beige silk kurta under a dark brown bundi. A Mont Blanc pen shone from his breast pocket.

Mont Blancs and Khadi, that was what made you in, that was what made you appear intellectual, committed, and rich at the same time. I must have been the only man in that party who did not possess a Mont Blanc pen. I still believed in the old reliability of a Parker 51. I suppose people must have thought that odd or quaint or eccentric—anything but up with the times.

The minute they walked in I went off to the veranda with my drink. There was a bonfire out there and another set of people. I didn't need to confront Rajiv and Mina and I didn't need to let all the others know about us and give them the pleasure of watching me make fumbling bloody drawing-room conversation with her and her lover. So I stayed out there, watching the planes land and talking to whoever came and sat next to me on the rounded cane chairs around the bonfire. I sat and listened to the man who I thought was the most valuable man of the evening, a diplomat from Belarus. His introduction was sudden and strange— 'I am from White Russia,' he said and immediately brought up images of the Russian civil war, the times of the revolution, blood on the pristine white endless snow, the images that had haunted me as a child ever since I stealthily and with thumping heart read a few pages from a Maxim Gorky book bound in leather the colour of old blood.

All evening he strummed a guitar easily around the bonfire for a small group and sang old Russian songs that reminded me of all sorts of strange things—of golden corn, of long trains, of dancing in circles around a fire in the snow and girls with smiling, glinting faces, bright red roses on the black scarves on their heads. He sang as if he was singing to himself, oblivious of the group that slowly became larger and people stood around when there were no more cane chairs to go around.

His singing made me want to cry.

I am amazed at the things that make me want to cry nowadays. A flash of a smile, the glint of youth on a cheek, two foolish young lovers looking at each other in a bus, a man coming home with a briefcase and a shopping bag with that look on his face that he is going to be with his family and have his evening tea, the way Joy used to clean up her desk in the evening as if she was never going to come back to it, the memory of walking with my mother on a sunny chequerboard floor of marble while people around us celebrated the festival of Basant in saffron kurtas and turbans and ate saffron rice'. . . Little strange things that make me want to sit down, hold my head in my hands and cry. I suppose that it is something within me that is doing it. It may well be that the diplomat from Belarus has already forgotten all about the haunting beauty of his own song. But I will remember it for a long time, like all those tucked away moments that flash across my mind in my dismal solitude . . . I do not dare call it loneliness . . . loneliness on this scale would be death.

I took another drink and let those tunes and words float around me, swirl and dance and twist and pull out the venom, the sadness, the dark swathes of grief that had settled in somewhere deep within. And if that worked, if that worked even for a night, I would have knelt down and kissed the singer's hands. I would have prayed that his tunes freeze into gold and his words become magic itself.

Once or twice, I glanced through the lace curtains into the large room inside and I saw Mina dancing with Rajiv. She had always danced with Rajiv, even in the old days and I had always known that there was a physical chemistry between them that they expressed by dancing together whenever they could. Her body was taut with energy, her chin with the gentle cleft I knew so well was thrust out towards him and there was genuine laughter in her dark eyes. I was never any good at dancing. I stepped on her toes every time I tried to do a slow dance with her or I moved too fast and I did not practice when we were alone. I suppose she was happy about that now; she did not need to practice with Rajiv in private.

And then Rajiv came out on the terrace, pulling out a cigarette elegantly from a silver case. He spent some time with me, as if he was holding my hand and saying that he was sorry for all that had happened. This was the kind of brassy cool that had always set him off from me, the almost indecent ability to do what he wanted and to hell with the world. His solicitous nonchalance appeared to indicate not that he had walked off with my wife but that he had taken a newspaper from my room without asking me. It was strange. I couldn't just get up and walk away; I couldn't slam my fist into the chocolate of his good looks. I had known him for years, even before I had got married to Mina. Rajiv was one of the first people who had entered that lost diary a long time ago.

9

He entered that diary when I came back from Bombay, running away from the rum-filled evenings of Sunshine Terrace, disillusioned with the grief that fuelled Rohini's desperate laughter, laden with guilt for having added to it, sobered by the loss of my first battle in the cut and thrust of the business world.

I spent a lot of time walking around Connaught Place those days, looking for a job, the right kind of job. I haunted the usual places that were considered 'in' those days—Volga and Wengers, Standard and Bankura—for lunch or coffee or gossip. It was over a lunch of kathi kababs with fresh mint chutney at Bankura that I first met Rajiv. He was with a man I had sought out when I toyed briefly with the romantic notion of joining a tea garden, drawn by images of white linens, early morning tennis games, motorcycle tours around the moist green hills. The man was a tea executive with some sort of princely background. He was quiet, distinguished, well bred, with a neat silk scarf, a smart blazer and a polite manner. He told me things that put me off the tea industry forever. He talked about generations of slaves who had worked in the tea gardens, exhorted to pluck and prune by British tea managers on horseback, and of present-day workers who slogged and sweated for a pittance. He wasn't trying to attract me to the tea gardens; in fact, he was fed up himself. He wanted to become a journalist and that was why he in turn was meeting up with Rajiv, an old friend from school. We realized this half way through the lunch and had a good laugh. I liked Rajiv at that moment. He laughed out loud and clear, like a man with a large heart and a clean conscience. A large enough heart, I was to later discover, to house my wife, and a clean enough conscience to still talk to me.

He was then a cub reporter in an evening daily at a few hundred rupees a month, having got a diploma from the Dateline School of Journalism at the end of Punchkuian Road. I was without a job. I think it was our shared near-penury that made us friends. He told me several times about his most interesting assignment. He chose six famous personalities—a dancer, a radio commentator, the skipper of the national hockey team, a poet, an Opposition politician and a celebrity cartoonist—and left each of them with a shattering question: What would you do if you had only twenty-four hours to live? When he returned the next day, he got quite a mixed bag. I have forgotten all the answers that he got except that of the famous dancer. She said that she would have a good massage, drink chilled white wine and make love for twenty-four hours. I remember that answer because it excited me as it had excited Rajiv. He led his story with that quote and won a formal letter of praise from the editor. He called me, and along with a couple of girls who were also cub reporters, we celebrated with platefuls of hot gulab jamuns soaked in syrup.

Once in a while, for extra money, he did longer features for other magazines. One Sunday, bored and alone at home, I went with him to do a story on a retired Professor who promised perfect wives to all and sundry. His advertisements were everywhere—on school walls and bus stops, on tree trunks and paan shops, along the train tracks for a thousand miles from Delhi to Assam: '27 Rehgarhpura'—the advertisements screamed—'at least come and visit.'

The Professor sat in a roomy deserted house almost hidden behind a pile of postcards from far and wide. Peering at them closely through square spectacles balanced on the bridge of his nose, he sorted them out meticulously in piles around his desk. Brahmins separate from Vaishyas, Khatris separate from Aroras, Mangliks separate from everyone else. Then he made minute notes on each one of them in the small neat handwriting that should rightly have belonged to an accounts clerk. Notes about income, complexion, demands for bicycle, scooter or car, background of science or arts education, number of brothers and sisters, married or unmarried ... He called us on the evening reserved for Brahmins. We watched him go from family to family, whispering lies and exaggerations, promising eternal happiness to the dozens gathered there amidst the wooden benches, and in the street outside, under the yellow light of the street bulbs, and some even in the shadows where the gutter pigs lay. I wonder how many of those marriages worked out and how many of those which worked out, lasted. Perhaps if we had gone through him, Mina and I, the Professor would have seen the ultimate futility of our marriage straightaway. Perhaps he would have handed her to Rajiv right then and saved everybody all this trouble. Here is the better man, the Professor would have told Mina, pointing out Rajiv, as he stood calmly. This man will truly take care of you, always bring home sufficient money, not be torn by doubts and fears, and what's more important, will give you the full joy of the marital bed. Do not go that way, he would have continued, pointing me out slyly, with just a glance towards me. That way lies bitterness, vacillation, weakness, divorce ...

Anyhow, that story of Rajiv's became a big one and reached the cover of a youth magazine run by a dyspeptic woman with heavily dyed hair and badly smudged kohl. She showed him a world that he entered wide-eyed, then made his own. That was his victory.

Yes, I have known Rajiv since those days, and when he came out on the terrace after dancing with Mina, we didn't need to talk much. It was difficult for me to be angry with him even though he was now living with my wife of fourteen years, and I suppose he understood that and I suppose that made him feel even worse about all that had happened. And of course that made me feel better.

10

I never forgot that night at 27 Rehgarhpura because I thought of it every time I looked out of my office window into the backyard of Connaught Place—the ugly, paan-stained, crumbling world of stores, garages, urinals and workshops. Far below, for several years after our visit, I could see the exhortations to go to 27 Rehgarhpura painted in bold black on the sick yellow walls and I knew that the old professor was still going strong. And then, overnight, the signs got painted over and election posters took their place.

From that window I could also see several trucks that belonged to the Coke factory except that it was not really Coke but something pretty near it. Almost the real thing. I could look into Shankar Market, the catacomb of dingy shops with cement verandas and unending arches. Every inch of those verandas was overflowing with things—plastic mugs, hairpins, underwear, false hair buns, locks and keys, ballpoint pens, watchstraps. A crazed world of the cheap, the second-hand, the cut-throat. I hardly ever went there. It was enough that once in a while I could bear to glance at it from my office window, eight floors up on high.

Some days I looked more through that window than on others. Some days I did not look inwards, at the office. Some days were just awful. Basu got to be too much.

I never liked Basu at all, not for one day of the five years that we worked together. I didn't like the fact that he was my superior and that at the end of every quarter, he wrote a report on me—on my initiative, my ability to take decisions, to manage a team, to entertain and socialize, even on my bloody linguistic ability. And in that last paragraph of those two pages he would recommend what direction I should take to become a better Manager of Public Relations, a greater asset to the Organization, a more useful cog in his Great Wheel. I always felt in my bones that no matter what the Board had decided, I was the one who was his superior, that if anybody had to give somebody else a certificate and a direction for further development, I should be giving it to Mr Shantanu Basu. Mr Basu who had quietly parked his wife of twenty some years in a flat on the other side of the Yamuna and moved in with thirty-two-year-old Neeta (surname unknown), the Mr Basu who during the emergency in 1975 had actually reported on his friends in college to the police, the Mr Basu who even now fraudulently increased the hours he was on tour just to make that extra half day of allowance. I wouldn't have needed that long paragraph at the end. I would have dismissed him in short, one-word judgements.

Direction—downwards.

Utility—zilch.

Sociability—negligible.

And so on.

Basu wanted badly to fit into the image of the private sector type, or what he imagined was the private sector type. That was because he spent twenty-two years in the Government before he took premature retirement and joined our company. To be part of the great historic sweep of economic liberalization that had suddenly made everything different, he would have said. But we all knew that he had done it simply to make more money. He was always trying to pretend that he was not a Government type, not a babu, no red tape, no delays, let's meet all the objectives in sharp bullet points, let's have brainstorming sessions, let's call each other by first names. That's the one that really got me. Having to call him Shantanu. Once he even told me—Just call me Shanty my man.

Shanty! My man!

Like hell!

He tried hard to convince me that the day he took premature retirement he had packed up all his Government baggage, all the survival skills and twist and slime that had combined to make him Additional Director General in the Directorate of Advertising and Visual Publicity, and thrown it out of the cooler-crowded third floor of the PTI building. But clearly he had kept all his safari suits, gray and brown and white, teri-wool in winter, teri-cot in summer, all stitched in a tiny shop in the middle circle of Connaught Place that he kept talking about but wouldn't reveal the address. Great tailors, third generation, he would pointedly say, and leave it at that.

He read a lot of magazines on corporate management, in a rush to make up for those lost twenty-two years in which he had only read government files with their green note sheets, tags and flags. There are some people who believe in everything they read in magazines. He had been reading up about stress management in the workplace during those last weeks. One day he got bean balls issued to everyone—purple, red, yellow, bright green bean balls in a net casing to squeeze in case you felt stressed. I wondered what was coming next. I should have known.

He got in to office one day soon after the bean ball morning and announced at the door that he had found the best way of managing stress, something that would now make our world one of smiling, laughing, stress-free happy people. Laughter—the best medicine. Just stand up and laugh if you are feeling stressed out. Or laugh anyway about sixteen times a day. Look into the nearest potted plant and laugh. Look out of the window at the row of urinals far below and laugh. Not just smile self-consciously to yourself but laugh out loud, guffaw. And he stood there with his steel gray safari suit and his oily thick salt-and-pepper hair and let out a huge bellow at nothing in particular.

'Nothing like that to relax one,' he said. 'And God save the man now who doesn't laugh. I want to hear laughter resounding at least every half an hour in this office. I want you all to chill out and to play it really cool.'

Indeed! He could go straight to hell. Shanty, old boy, I thought, I was not going to laugh at my computer screen. I was suffering. Besides, I always liked my stress. It was all that I had left. It gave me my energy and my zing. In the language of Basu's magazines, it worked for me. So please, I told Mr Basu silently, let me keep my keyed-up nerves and sharp edges while you laugh away yours.

He knew I didn't like him. And he knew that I knew that he had his knife in me and was only waiting for the chance to twist it.

Some days I waited for him to do the final wrenching, gut-tearing twist and be over with it so that we could all go home and watch cricket on television or something. On other days I wanted to walk up to him, put my knee in his balls, if he still had any—the office joke was that Neeta had locked them up in a safe-deposit box—and turn the knife in his guts instead and walk to the nearest police station and turn myself in.

Yes, some days were bad.

11

The breakfast that is served in this train is a grimy mess. A rolled-up omelette fried in too much oil and laced with the smell of cheap plastic, two slices of tasteless bread, a round potato chop, two packets of tomato sauce that do not tear at the corner where they are meant to, and a cup of weak coffee. But still, it provides me with something to do while I wait for the train to stop so that I can get up and stretch my legs. On the hard wooden upper berths of the third-class compartments of the old days, the berths meant for suitcases and bulging bedrolls and baskets of fruit and Eagle flasks of water, I could stretch out fearlessly. But now I can only shift and flex and wait for the train to stop at Saharanpur.

I remember Saharanpur for its smells, the sharp smell of oil on raw leather, the sweet smell of sugarcane being cut in the sun, the thick smell of jaggery being made. And for the thousands of droning black flies, fattened on the sugarcane juice, drowsy in the heat. I remember stopping there on one of our trips in the car from Dehradun to Delhi, the trips that came up whenever my father had a meeting in Delhi and we all packed into the staff car to spend a couple of days with my grandmother and my endless army of aunts and uncles and cousins. We bought rough leather sandals there, unable to believe our luck at the price for which they were sold to us. Rough thick slip-ons like the ones the farmers wore, soaked in oil, the darkened leather made to look like juicy mango paper.

The dark green of the trees in the drops beyond the rail line today is the dark green of those car journeys when we stopped at roadside orchards and watched the children swinging from the ancient mango trees. The branches loaded with the saharni mangoes, the ones I love for that unexpected last-minute tang at the back of the throat. Rounded and smaller than the safeda, less classy than the dussehri and not quite as authentic as the langra or the chausa—the saharni, the modest fruit, my favourite.

I haven't eaten that kind of mango for years. In fact, I haven't eaten any mango the right way for years, sitting on a string cot under the dark green shade, reaching out for a bucketful of mangoes cooled in the water of a hand pump, halfway between two towns. Mangoes are not good for me any more. Just like most other good things in life. They are too sweet, they fall in the narrowest, topmost part of the pyramid—along with chocolates and cakes and wine—in the diabetic magazines, the kind that I have started looking at, almost surreptitiously, ever since my blood tests at Dr Rao's clinic. Something has to happen at this age, Mina used to say, or all of us would live forever.

I have no intention of living forever, God forbid. I had said as much to Dr Rao in my most cynical dry voice as he stared grimly at my report, the result of the analysis of my scarlet blood. Half a test tube on an empty stomach and half a test tube after I had gone to the hospital canteen and eaten two toasts, pale yellow scrambled eggs and a cup of tea without sugar on a square table with a white sun mica top. Through the wire mesh of the canteen window, I had stared at the patch of dusty grass, unwatered and uncared for, but somehow always there, familiar and constant, and then I had found myself muttering something about the world being all right as long as men like Dr Rao were around. He'd been coming to this hospital every Tuesday and Friday for years now, seeing the patients who no longer went all the way to his crowded clinic in Karolbagh.

Even I hadn't been to his Karolbagh clinic for many years. Not since the time he had shifted out of the extended garage with its three rows of benches to a nearby house. But there had been many childhood visits to that garage to play out the painful summer ritual of the typhoid, cholera and paratyphoid injections— the deathly sounding TABC—produced by Bengal Chemicals and bought from the chemist's shop, just across the circle from the garage clinic, that smelt overwhelmingly of gripe water. After the injections and before the painful lumps formed in our arms and the sick feeling of rising fever began as a dull pain in the head and made us want to lie down, we would step across the road from the clinic into another shop and look at the gold and blue fish in the aquariums flitting about in the bubbling water.

Dr Rao had a sure touch. He was known all over Delhi for the way he gave an injection by first throwing the needle almost casually into the flesh and then attaching the syringe. It was over before you knew that it had begun, while you still crouched on the narrow examining bed. Then he would light up his Red & White cigarette and call for the next patient. Not all his patients or their woes that he witnessed had been able to make old Rao give up his beloved Red & White cigarettes, and those days it seemed he would smoke himself away one day into thin air. But nothing happened to him until one day his daughter got a viral infection in the morning and was dead by the evening. He stopped smoking then and I don't know what else must have happened to him.

As he pored over my report now, he was nearly blind. But the verdict was still as sure as ever. If I didn't want to be put on medicines immediately, if I didn't want my heart to seize up on me suddenly or my arteries choked or my kidneys destroyed, if I didn't want to go blind like him and have my toes chopped off to prevent gangrene, I had better get a hold on myself and my sugar levels. In his rasping voice, with edges like an old-fashioned saw, he told me all sorts of things to do and not to do but the most important thing was exercise, 'at least twenty minutes five times a week until you are aerobic.'

The man who sold me the treadmill, the thing that would hereafter ensure that I went aerobic five times a week, was a strange sort of salesman, an intellectual, I thought, in the wrong job. I have always felt a deep sympathy for people in the wrong job. I was part of the brotherhood, of men doomed to do work that sickened them to begin with. That salesman should have been in some green-lawned, fabulously-domed university, walking hurriedly through hallowed corridors, nodding absent-mindedly to passing students, pondering the abstruse questions of why and why not, searching at night through the telescope of his mind for answers from an even lonelier distance. Instead, life had made him a salesman of exercise equipment in a fast expanding sports shop in Lodhi market, constrained only by the presence of a tailor and a drycleaner on either side of the shop. As he showed me the exercise bikes and treadmills, he thought and debated, pushing back his heavy black square spectacles from the tip of his nose where they kept dropping, tortured himself into knots over every innocent query of mine, knocked his toes against nonchalant bar-bells, winced and swore. But he sold me a treadmill, threw in a ten per cent discount and immediately made it up by also persuading me to sign on a two-year maintenance contract. Afterwards, he sighed, smiled and made a little bow, almost as if apologizing for having stepped on my toes in a crowded bus.

As I walked out of the shop, I filed him away in my head as a member of the inner coterie, the board of directors, the kitchen cabinet of the Association of Men in Wrong Jobs. Poor chap, I thought as I half pushed, half threw the treadmill box into the back of the car with the help of the shop assistant. A part of it stuck out and the boot wouldn't shut but it was too heavy to fall out. And I would have to use it, having gone to all that effort to buy it. Maybe somehow it would stave off the silent killer that had begun, sweetly, to eat my heart out from the inside.

Twenty minutes a day, Dr Rao had said, and it hadn't sounded all that much. I kept at it for a few days, testing my blood each morning, exercising every evening, watching the reading drop point by point on the small grey glucometer. Then something gave way and I couldn't keep at it any more. The whole thing began to make me immensely sad and lonely. The loneliness of the long distance runner, stepping blithely and lightly through open vistas, like a cheetah in the bush, health oozing out of every taut muscle, is nothing compared to the loneliness of a diabetic on a treadmill. This is a dreadful, gnawing, sick and secret loneliness. It is uphill all the way, uphill against thoughts of all that is nice and sweet and tasty and from which one is cut off by an invisible barrier. Behind this barrier can be seen rows of chocolates and melting cakes and hot gulab jamuns and mugs of frothing beer moving in charmed arcs to young ruby red lips. Or fleshy French fries dipped in mustard sauce or strawberry milkshake surging thickly through the straw or good wine that warms the sides of the mouth just to look at it. I know now that it was the wrong way of looking at things. I should have been all geared up to 'tackle it', counting calories and carbohydrates and fibre content, a model patient, obedient and responsive and successful. Then Dr Rao would not have been able to say dryly: 'Nature of the beast, onto medicines now.' Instead of waiting to hit the sickbed, alone and full of self-pity, I should have made better use of that treadmill, had it serviced free as part of the contract, run on it morning and evening. Instead, I allowed Balram to make it a convenient place to dry my underwear.

Mina would have predicted this on day one. She would have been surprised by how long I actually kept at it. Perhaps I have always handled things wrongly, just that little bit.

Vijay Singh, the man in the next seat, has in sharp contrast, always handled things right. Yes, we are talking now. I couldn't hold out any longer, I had to go so I had to ask him to kindly fold up his meal tray. He did that with alacrity, grateful to me for this opportunity to start talking. Now he rushes, as he must tell me all in the few minutes before we reach Saharanpur.

'In India, in Saharanpur, this uniform works like magic. Nobody will be able to fool me, they will not overcharge me for the tonga, they will salute me as I leave the station, they will not even check my ticket. Of course I have a ticket. Money—money is no longer a problem, you see. God has given me more than enough and I have not wasted one pound, not one pound.'

He pins up a brass badge on his chest. Security officer, it says in a gentle curve.

'London Underground, you know. I check the piling. My company puts in the iron pillars filled with concrete into the ground so that the earth does not shift with the moving trains. I check them. Very hard work, we have to be underground many many hours. But without hard work, I ask you, is there any way out?'

I look at his black uniform, incongruous in this weather, his thick double-soled Oxford shoes upto his ankles, his ID card that he has pulled out of his breast pocket as if to prove to me that he is indeed telling the truth.

He didn't reach London in a day. It was a long way from Saharanpur. He has worked all over the world—in Abadan, Muscat, Norway. And in London he has lived alone for nine years. He hasn't bought a car, not taken a mortgage on a house, not taken his family to London. No smoking, no drinking, absolutely no women. Instead he saves a thousand pounds per month and just translate that into rupees and you have two houses in Saharanpur, double storeyed, three sons educated, two daughters ready for marriage this month. He cooks his own food in London, the same old Indian way, buys vegetables where they are cheap, does not believe in meat, has no friends at all.

He has done it all the right way, firmly, decisively. And when he reaches his house in Saharanpur, gets off the tonga amidst the salutes and the bows, hands out gifts bought in clearance sales, he will bask in the love of his wife, respect of his children, envy of his neighbours.

I salute you, Vijay Singh. I envy you. I wish I too could have done things the right way.

SAHARANPUR

1

The train slides in smoothly into the ten o'clock torpor that has fallen with the inevitability of a shroud over the Saharanpur railway station. The door opens and the warm air rushes in; the late summer is still here. Everybody in the cabin wants to step out but Vijay Singh is out first, signalling haughtily to a coolie to carry his two suitcases. He grips my hand with both of his, thanks me, tells me he has enjoyed our journey together and swaggers off. I hold myself back and later, five minutes of the twenty-minute stop already gone, walk out into the smell of coal, dung and mangoes that floats over the platform, poisoning the chrome yellow sunshine.

From where I stand, at the edge of the rail lines, the platform is long and unfriendly. A trolley behind me sells the usual junk sold on all railway platforms—magazines, dak editions of newspapers, water bottles, packs of playing cards, nail cutters, key chains. An old woman, her skin shrivelled into a thousand deep lines, promises me eternal happiness with her scurvy-ridden tongue and toothless mouth if I throw her a coin. Eternal happiness, no less, at great discount, everything must go, come one come all. I give her a coin and walk on, not waiting for her to deliver on her improbable part of the deal.

When they married us, Mina and I, at ten o'clock in the morning, in the curtained-off veranda of an Armed Services club, they promised us eternal happiness too. That promise was there in everything, in the scriptures, in the blessings of the trembling grandparents, in the smell of marigolds around my neck and the rose petals crushed under our feet. Then everybody left us holding that promise, already sounding cheap and hollow like something bought in a hurry at a discount, and rushed into the hall to devour the butter chicken, naans, saag paneer and the rest of it.

Only three months earlier I had parked the family car in front of a block of flats in Rabindra Nagar. My father had looked up quickly at the yellow first-floor flat and nodded with approval.

'D-I, fairly senior. But not too senior.'

'Let's see the girl,' was my mother's gentle reminder that we should focus on only the most essential issue. She was happy that I had agreed to come along at all, that I had put the Rohini episode behind me. She did not want any extraneous considerations to now queer the pitch. It had, in any case, taken her several weeks of patient nudging to get my father and me back on talking terms.

The girl, when we saw her, was pleasant and pretty. Young and smiling tentatively, dressed in a pale yellow salwar kameez, her freshly washed hair bouncing on her shoulders. She talked little. She concentrated on helping her mother serve the tea on the dining table for six that occupied half of the room. The smouldering black of her eyes, accentuated by long lines of kohl, and her full lips attracted me.

'Mina made these little pizzas,' her mother said proudly as she placed the tiny rectangular pizzas in our plates.

Then she turned to the rasgollas.

'Of course these are all from the market. There's a very nice shop in Khan Market and the rasgollas are best, fresh and soft, if you get them just at four in the afternoon.'

We ate and we talked, munching our way through the carefully guided conversation.

'Aftab's job really keeps him busy. You know these managerial positions in the private sector are far more demanding than our government jobs,' my father told Mina's father who nodded, agreeing readily.

'Yes of course, just look at me. If I had been in the private sector, I would never have got the time to build our own house. It's just about to be finished. Sector 15 in Noida.'

I turned to the cashew nuts, salted and crisp, and heard the two fathers make veiled statements about their status, about their cars, about their houses, about their contacts. All the time I watched Mina's pale hands, trembling slightly, shaking the silver of her bangles. Once or twice I caught her eye and she quickly looked away. When that evening ended, we were all sufficiently undecided to agree that I should drop in once again the same week, 'so that the two young people have a chance to talk to each other—that's how they need to do it in this day and age.'

We met twice again in quick succession, half excited, somewhat nervous. Once, sitting on the cream sofa in that same room, I watched Mina play with the corner of her tie-and-dye dupatta and explained to her what I did in my office and she told me what she had studied and the exams that she still had to take in four months' time. The second time, we walked up and down the terrace of her flat, searching for a dim understanding of each other as the evening birds flew home towards the old trees of Lodhi Garden and the last rays of the sun scraped the tops of the tombs that rose above the trees. After that, largely because I could not come up with any major objection, I told my father that if everybody else was happy about it, we could go ahead with the marriage. I wrote a letter to Rohini one of those nights telling her how I had met Mina and posted it at the Jorbagh post office just behind the old red building of the Met office.

Too many people, besides Vijay Singh, have got off at Saharanpur. I did not expect them to. I had gotten used to them. I wanted them to go with me till the end of the journey, until we reached the familiar platform from where I would be able to find my own way, unaided and unaccompanied. The three ice-blue vacant seats in my row tell me that they just had to go their way, like I have to go mine, like Mina and Rajiv have gone theirs, like Rohini went so many years ago.

Three hours together in a train and we get used to people. We get used to so much—the fading colours of a carpet, the comforting green of a plant, the smell of food cooking, songs from the servants' quarters while breakfast is being made, the dog curled over the front mat with one ear cocked for a faraway sound, the hiss in the tap as we wait for the water at four o'clock on summer afternoons, the low voltage . . . even the tartar that gathers insidiously around our teeth. It does not matter whether we like these things or not, whether we would like them to change or not . . . we simply get used to them.

I look beyond the vacant seats. There is a group of youngsters sitting behind me since Delhi. They are debating amongst themselves whether they would like to sing songs. I think they will, once one of them finds the courage to start. It is that first step that is important.

About two years ago, when the promise of eternal happiness was finally discarded as empty, Mina first moved into that guest room. She had told me all then—that she and Rajiv had been out for dinner when I was out of town, that they had sat under a full moon on broad sandstone steps listening to the buzz of insects in the trees. He had begged her for her love, he had held her hand, squeezing it so that her ring hurt between her fingers. He had bravely leaned over and kissed her on her cheek and finally she had given in to the strong physical attraction she had always felt for him. In the morning, I was sure, she must have felt guilty, all wrong, but by then it was done. Mina had tasted earthy physical satisfaction, in a way that for one reason or the other, she had not found in my arms.

That's when I failed to do the right thing. I should have called up Rajiv. No, not shot him in his bathtub, but called him and made them sit together in front of me and screamed at them for having betrayed me together. It would have all been sorted out one way or the other. Instead, I slunk away; I played the decent man. I let Mina stay on, thinking that it would all be fine again, at least as fine as before. I let Rajiv call her, he even began again to drop in as if nothing had really happened. Wasn't that how Naini and Prashant had been? Even after their divorce they took vacations together, went for movies together, still had a joint bank account. And we weren't even divorced. That's when I chickened out . . . or perhaps I pretended that this would be best for Ankur.

I kept my anger, my humiliation mostly to myself. It all didn't seem to amount to much except that it was the first step. After that it was all downhill, though at times we did not notice it. We gradually stopped being a couple; we stopped doing all those ordinary things that couples do in their own ways—going for a movie to a cinema hall, not a video rental, every Friday night. Playing scrabble on rainy afternoons making words that had meaning only for us, like squish and toot and crady. Sharing cups of black coffee from our favourite mugs. We were together only because we were married.

So when Mina finally told me over that lunch at Triveni that she was leaving me for Rajiv, there was nothing too sudden about it. My vanity was hurt, my great male ego was shattered, but the betrayal was already two years old. I was used to it. Over those two years, I had, even unknown to myself, been preparing myself for the last step. And let me confess that in those two years I too betrayed the empty promise of our marriage, though only once, when in a distant town, on a heavenly night, I kissed a strange girl with orange lipstick on a lonely bridge and never met her again.

The youngsters behind me are passing around pineapple pastries, another one of those things that I cannot eat any more. I am jealous of their ability to eat freely and I yearn to feel the taste of the thick cream and the crunchy pineapple, but I am not jealous of their youth or their inexperience or their whole foolishness. They have so much to learn yet, too much to get hurt over, be ashamed about. They are excited that the train is moving fast again. They say that this train will not stop in too many places after Saharanpur. Only at Roorkee and Haridwar.

There is a girl in the group, a girl in black clothes that heighten her transparent faraway beauty. She jogs a distant memory of someone I met after Rohini. That girl had the same wide-eyed innocent look and she liked me because I could make her laugh. On the evenings when I had nothing much to do, tired of looking for a good job in Delhi, on the evenings of the days of waiting, empty summer evenings without a hint of a breeze, I sought her out. Only to see whether I could, day after day, make her laugh. She laughed under the jamun trees, in the dark, on the damp grass. I nuzzled against the perfume on her neck. There was never much talk, no promise, no opening for regret. Only the kisses, quiet and sad, almost without passion, as if they were recompense for an evening of laughter. And at the end of that summer, when the rains came down and we could no longer sit under the jamun trees, that was the time I found my job and then went with my parents to see Mina. Those evenings came to an end, but still, as I watch that girl a few rows behind me, I think of laughter under the jamun trees.

2

Yellow houses. Squat, tired yellow houses. At the far edge of Saharanpur, at the fringe of the railway colony, where the mango trees meet the sugarcane fields. Houses of clerks and engine drivers, of accountants and inspectors. Houses that need to be painted; the barbed wire fences that keep out the cows and the dogs need to be replaced. Four houses to a block. The ones on the top floor have the terrace where the billowing clothes—the cotton sarees, the blouses, the childrens' shorts, the white kurtas and the vests and underwear that have lost their shape—are hung out to dry on the line tied to the pipe on the metal cistern at one end and the TV antenna at the other. The ground-floor flats have their little gardens, with occasional flowers in mud pots, tin cans, cracked plastic buckets. Here the clothes are hung out to dry in the little patch at the back, where the overgrowing grass rushes into the bramble. If it were winter, there would be string cots stretched out in front where the women would sit and gossip and eat oranges after lunch, watching, from the corners of their eyes, the children playing near the pond in which the buffaloes stood shoulder deep.

I have lived long in such yellow houses, big and small, whenever my father was posted in Delhi. They are part of the life of a Government servant, like my father, who was a very busy Government servant. He always told us that and that was what I saw whenever I went to his office to get true copies of certificates attested before the days of the photocopier. Various peons stood guard outside his office throughout my childhood, holding him away from me while I grew up. But they always did it kindly. Pritam Singh, who put me on his cycle bar when he came to pick me up from kindergarten. On the day of the solar eclipse he told me not to look at the sun. Old Mirchu Ram, who came home in the mornings to double up as a cook. He made chapattis for me in different shapes and sizes. Chappatis as milk-laden cows, chappatis as crescent moons, chappatis as tongas and cycle-rickshaws. And Nathu Ram, who covered my books with thick brown paper and stuck on the name labels with office glue. And half a dozen others. They were the men I had to pass when I went to my father's offices. Offices in Delhi and Nangal and Dehradun, wherever the work of hydroelectric dams or oil exploration took him with its paraphernalia of canals and reservoirs and drilling and blasting and yellow-helmeted executive engineers in their old Ford pick-up vans. Offices with revolving leather chairs, revolving bookshelves, glass paperweights and water glasses covered with little crocheted cloth with red, blue and yellow beads at the edges to weigh it down. And charts, always charts showing the spending of budgets, the countdown of days, the ebb and flow of water. In these offices he held those magical mysterious things—meetings. Long-drawn-out, exhausting, tense meetings that we heard about after they were long over, and that ultimately gave him high blood pressure.

All this kept him busy for thirty years. And in his way he must have moved up in life. For we moved into bigger and bigger houses. We started opposite Safdarjang hospital. I do not remember much of it except what I can see in those little black-and-white photographs. I haven't looked at them for years, but somewhere in my childhood days I have looked at them so hard and so often, that I don't need to look at them any more. Photographs mostly with me at the centre in a little pram. My mother never forgave herself for the fact that she left it outside a shop and it was stolen. Her only consolation was that I, her only son, was not stolen with it. In later photographs that pram was replaced with a buggy, with large wheels and a hood like the real British buggies. And all the people in those photographs, those strange well-remembered faces, those vanished cousins and their vanished childhoods, lost to wars, divorces, jobs and heart attacks. Those long dead grandparents and their brothers and sisters who once seemed so close and to whom one is as indifferent now as one may be to a dinosaur. Those servants who held my buggy so proudly and one day were asked to leave the house because they grew too proud to answer my mother if she called. Those photographs are all I remember of the first yellow house except for one clear memory of a clean blue sky against a window with rounded iron bars and a crow on a branch outside the window.

The next house that I remember had a large mango tree in its front garden and a dilapidated chicken coop in its backyard. Lizards lived happily in the gray-cemented bathroom and flicked their tongues and caught little insects on the edges of the dim tube lights. I hated those lizards, they kept me awake at nights, and years later in my college hostel I would sleep with my door and windows closed on the hottest summer night just to keep them from coming in at night from the hot roof. And later on still, Mina always laughed at me, in that infectious giggly way that she has, when I looked into both legs of my trousers or pyjamas before wearing them. I told her it was fear of lizards but she told me I was mad. As a boy I wanted to be like my friend Shivi, in the house across the lawn. He had an air pistol and the day he got it he shot three lizards in his house and splattered their remains all over the walls.

Just before I was to leave the University and go away to Bombay, my father was posted back to Delhi, a year before he retired. That was the last big house, with an extra bedroom, an extra bathroom and a much larger back veranda with a small washbasin. I liked to wash my face at that washbasin in the cold mornings and stare out at Ring Road and the huge intersection that was one of the first in Delhi to get the high traffic lights and the sweeping lanes for the free left turns. In the early morning, Delhi could still be romantic and beautiful with the bougainvillea in the road dividers and cyclists with huge milk cans tied to heavy carriers coming in from the villages. With that house came the red telephone, a sleek, flat instrument that purred gently and dialled smoothly and quickly. My mother loved that red telephone and it would be her constant attempt throughout her life never to be without a red telephone instrument again. One had to be important to be issued anything other than the standard black heavy monster with which we had grown up. Even today she has a red telephone in her apartment. She kept it there after my father retired, even after he died, fighting fiercely with the telephone department. 'You cannot take it away once it has been given,' she told them. 'It shows the level at which he has retired. In Government you never lose the level that you have reached once.' She has kept it there through an expert combination of bullying and flattering successive lots of engineers, supervisors and linesmen until they all gave up and decided it was better for everybody concerned to let her keep it.

I hate all those yellow houses now, big or small. I cannot bear to look at them any more and I try not to pass those colonies if I can help it. The houses that once seemed stately and prestigious look run-down; the men and women who live there and go to office in car pools and chartered buses, don't appear so hard-working, honest and important any more. Merely petty, scheming and irrelevant. They have run out of options, it seems, or out of the courage to choose. I know how they struggle to make ends meet, how they wait to get those houses, how they beseech and implore and then finally bribe officials to get their telephones installed, their plumbing changed, their coolers put up every summer and taken off when the rains come, how they dread the day that they will retire and have to leave those houses and move into tiny apartments in faraway housing societies. I know how the paint chips off the walls and how the servants' quarters are given out to families who will do three jobs in the house instead of paying rent—the sweeping, the utensils and the clothes. And if paid a little bit, the poor souls who cannot believe their luck at having found a roof over their heads in the middle of green-leafed Delhi and not in some distant colony from where they would have to cycle miles to work, those poor souls will also do the cooking and ironing.

And sometimes I think—oh horrible thought—that if I had joined the Civil Service, as I had dreamt for so many years as a child, I would have spent my life living in those yellow houses. In the predictable progression from D II to D I to C II and C I. Then the whole drama of my life, my years with Mina, the months after her departure, the day of Ankur's caesarian birth, Rajiv's insidious visits, would have been played out in a house with plain gray cement floors, lizards in the bathrooms, pale yellow doors with heavy black latches, windows with rounded iron bars, many servants living, fighting, breeding in the attached quarters, washing their clothes under the brass tap of the water tank on the terrace.

But all that did not happen because I did not make it to the civil service; I was not good enough.

3

I must confess that I tried very hard. Five years before the exam I bought six long notebooks and wrote on them in green ink— Civil Service. Slowly, over the evenings, as the thin tall trees stood silhouetted against the flaming sky and the smell of jasmine made the insects buzz excitedly, dozens of unrelated facts, from magazines and newspapers, were gathered in those notebooks. Population figures, male-female ratios, the state in India with the most milch animals, the composition of an integrated chip. Somewhere this was all expected to jell into a whole, for that big battle against thousands of candidates, for those few jobs at the end of the tunnel.

Later, in my postgraduate years, I continued the battle from Jubilee Hall. J-Hall stood at the edge of the University, from where it was obvious that one more step, another blissful year or two, and we would be out into the teeming world, struggling for existence and success beyond Mall Road. Among people who always seemed to be waiting for buses that never came or were too crowded to board, looking for relief in cold water from refrigerated carts at five paise a glass or eating desperate dinners on the pavement from wooden handcarts with round coil heaters. In the evenings we watched this world rush into the flats across the road, faceless rectangular little windows of light, all exactly the same except for their numbers, all with their twenty-one-inch TV sets and the Sunday evening movie, the small fridge in the drawing room with the white crocheted cover, the plastic flowers, the procession of sandalwood elephants on the shelf, the wedding photographs, the smell of oil frying in the kitchen and the relentless drumming of day after night after day.

But we were still on the sensible side of Mall Road. With its red brick walls and its long silent corridors, J-Hall put up a Horatious-like effort to ward off the real world. Everything was drowned in a stupor born of long numbing hours of study in the heat, day after day. J-Hall was like a factory in which about two hundred residents studied for the Civil Service and every year at least three or four, and sometimes more, made it to secure lifelong careers. The others carried on, pinning hopes on the next year. Some became veterans of the exam and then finally gave up and went back to farming.

Through the nightlong vigils, the canteen functioned efficiently. Pots of tea and soft French toasts were served on the lawns by the dwarf waiter who, everybody knew, was regularly sodomized by the other canteen boys. On these lawns we sat around in white kurta-pyjamas, asking each other questions, helping out with tips and notes, borrowing books and tactics until each night we finally fell asleep, the books still open. Sometimes a nerve would snap somewhere and a book would be flung across the room in sudden disgust, or a night show impulsively decided upon or a singing session launched. Once I saw an entire week's work being torn up in front of my eyes and left to float page by page into the night from a second-floor window.

I really pushed myself those last few weeks, sleeping only a few hours and taking frequent baths. The sight of books began to nauseate me and as the day approached it seemed to me that I hadn't prepared well enough, that despite the years of determined intent for this big effort, I had let it slacken in the end. With failing conviction I searched inside myself for a superhuman effort, a last dash that could still take me near the top of those other sixty odd thousand.

The exams lasted about ten days and passed as a fever does, leaving me drained. After the last day, at seven in the evening, with the ridge beyond the window already hidden in winter darkness, I fell into a helpless sleep. When I woke up I remember going out with some friends, our spirits high like in the old days. We bought tickets at black market rates for *Fiddler on the Roof*. We sat in the balcony and deliberately stretched out our legs. It gave us a strange thrill that every time shadowy women walked down the dark row, they nearly tripped over our legs. Then we had boiled eggs and tea from a roadside vendor while we waited for the night bus. We stood on the steps of the bus even though it was nearly empty and let the cold breeze catch our faces. And when we came back, we felt that we were once again seventeen and that nothing in the world mattered beyond that. The thoughts of competition, career, even continuous debates over women didn't bother us that night.

The results of the Civil Service exam came before I could go home for the holidays. I went to the high-domed building on Shahjahan Road. It was already getting dark and someone had trained the headlights of a car onto the huge black boards resting against the wall with the results stuck on them in long white sheets. Quickly I went through the list and then again, more carefully, with mounting despair. I was not in. The generous man with the headlights decided to go away and a sudden darkness descended on the courtyard. At the reception a night watchman switched on the lights and gave me a copy of the result sheets stitched together with a green shoelace. But nothing worked that night and as I came out of the building I vomited against the trunk of an old tree near the bus stop in the weak light of the fruit-juice stalls.

I could see my father's disappointment under his gentle concern. After all, he had taken the same exam, hadn't he, in much more trying circumstances. Three years after Partition, sitting as a refugee in temporary accommodation, amidst squabbling children and countless neighbours, battling with tragedy and loss. He had covered his head with a blanket and studied in the light that came through the bare threads and he had made it. And I with all the advantages of a Delhi University education, libraries and hostels and all the time in the world, had muffed it up.

Unable to do the right thing.

He asked me to try again, to make it to one of the Central services at least, maybe the railways or the accounts or the post and telegraphs, anything that would be secure, risk-free, with peons and housing, and at the end, a pension. When I told him that once was enough and I would try my luck in the private sector, he turned away in disapproval, muttering something under his breath about hiring and firing. And that was sixteen years ago, when neither he nor I had even dreamt of skunks like Basu, born and sheltered in the safety of the Government, and the treacherous traps they laid out in the byways of the private sector.

Sixteen years ago, I set myself up for all this: disaffection, defeat, this strange defiance against their world and my life. It could so easily have been otherwise.

4

They tell me, Rohini, that you can find virtually anything nowadays on the internet. It is simply not true. I looked for your phone number, your e-mail, your address every which way, tried every directory, every search engine, downloaded lists several pages long of people who shared your husband's name. But you were nowhere; you could have taught Greta Garbo a thing or two.

Did you look for me too? Ever? Or were you still angry with me? And if not, why was it so difficult for us to find each other? Or is it that we did not try hard enough? Perhaps we did not have the strength to test our hope, and so we waited. Like two lost stars in helpless, hopeless, flattened-out orbits that must know that once every few million years they would come together, or at least pass within sight of each other. We had to wait for the earth to turn; we could not, would not hurry.

And suddenly when I needed you the most, when things began to finally fall around me, I sought you out and you were there. A chance phone call, a casual enquiry about you and it was all possible. Chuck gave me your number. I could dial that number and talk to you ten times on the phone every day.

But I haven't spoken to you even once yet. Nor, for that matter, have you called. Just those e-mails. Are we scared of finding each other sounding old, tired, defeated? Are we scared of finding out what we both lost?

We shall speak when it is destined. I prefer to talk to you through our messages. Private, intimate messages, as if I were getting to know you again, innocently, deliberately. And nobody shall ever come to know. Except you, if it touches you the same way, still. If all these years have not completely wiped out what we felt for each other in the heat and the rain, by the long wall against which the sea broke and showered us with thin white spray and from where, in the morning, we could see the brown rocks left behind by the departing tide. I know that you remember it all with memories stronger than mine. You knew exactly what it was that you wanted, what you would have to do, what you would have to give up to get what you wanted. I only wanted it all, success and fame, love, respectability without giving up anything at all. It was I who let you down.

And in my messages, innocent rejoinders to yours, shorn of guilt since they are only replies, I shall try to tell you all. In my way I shall try to apologize, I shall try to make up, I shall even, given time and opportunity, make love to you again. And if it doesn't work then nothing, almost nothing will be lost.

Rohini's messages began to save my life. They were my secret allies against all that was lined up against me—Basu's scheming, Mina's badgering calls, the whisky-laden evenings.

Those messages made me want to go to office early in the morning, happy to be the first one there. I liked those twenty minutes to myself, before Joy and Basu and the whole world that they seemed to carry in their pockets came in. Those twenty minutes were like a meditation, the equivalent of a whole day of rest. I would take off my coat, hang it on the shoulders of my chair, switch on the computer and put on the water for the coffee while it loaded.

Password and user name and there it would be. The morning's inbox. 'Good morning'—that was the usual subject of Rohini's e-mail and I wouldn't want to open it till my coffee was ready, till my nerves had been steadied with that first sip. I would quickly go through the rest of the trash—the news bulletin, the routine queries about this and inconsequential that, the stock quotes. There would be several messages from Basu with red exclamation marks. All his messages had that red exclamation mark as if he was congenitally incapable of saying anything that was not important and urgent. I would leave those messages aside. I would need more than just a sip of freshly brewed coffee to handle them. Basu could stink.

One such morning, I came in from the rain, a late-April, out-of-season, sad sort of rain. That morning her message was short, written in a hurry, as if she had other things on her mind.

> *hi there*
>
> *it feels so great just to be in touch again. all these years and so many things later, to see your name on my screen, knowing that i can send you a message and you will get it immediately. thank god for e-mail. are you really busy in office? i mean your title sounds impressive. and is this address ok to write to you or does this go through your secretary or something? last year i was in bombay briefly— did you ever go back to bombay? i thought it was too crowded and all the old buildings are breaking down on marine drive. or is it just me getting old? more later, got to run . . .*
>
> *as always*
>
> *ro*

She would always be Ro to me, despite what I had done to her. And she had said that she would write more later. I took my cup of coffee to the window. Outside, the rain had become even harder and the leaves of the trees far below me were turning inside out, lime green instead of dark green, with the strong wind. I heard the sounds of the rising elevator. The world was arriving.

I knew that Joy would walk in, throwing her hair over her left shoulder in that nonchalant, supposedly sassy way of hers, slinging her bag over her shoulder and shaking her umbrella. She would see me and wish me and come in and hang around my desk for the few extra seconds, reaching out for some papers or for the coffee mug while all the time she would be trying to read my computer screen without actually looking at it. These things can be tough, Joy, I wanted to tell her. They can give you a headache that can ruin your entire day. And besides, even if you could read that message, you wouldn't make out much from it. You wouldn't even realize why Ro wants to know whether I went to Bombay again.

She wanted to know if I still remembered. If I remembered how it all happened, that brief bout of magic from our first meeting to my sudden departure, lasting only four months.

As if I could ever forget.

5

The train is rolling towards the clouds, moving imperceptibly away from the broad plains, towards taller trees, and finally the hills. The sky is beginning to darken; a heavy gray is creeping in at the edges. And then little drops of rain, slanting and splattering flat on the smudged green glass window as the train curves gently. I can no longer see the horizon. It must be raining harder than it seems.

On a winding track not far from the grassy slope leading down from the railway line, I see a man riding a bicycle, a tattered black umbrella over his shoulder. The umbrella bellows in the wind, slowing him down as he steers the heavy bicycle with his left hand. A few children are looking up at the sky, their hands raised in joy as the drops fall on their heads and bare chests. I want to be with them at the edge of the muddy pond. I want to walk on the narrow raised bund of the water channel that separates two sugarcane fields, barefoot and barebodied. I want to let the water wash over me until I am a child again, mindless and thoughtless, cleansed of the dust and smog of so many imperfect years.

I wonder what the rain has meant to you all these years, Rohini. Have you thought of anything at all as the clouds gathered and the day darkened all of a sudden under the thick trees in your garden? When the rain dripped from broad green leaves and brought them down in the backyard before their time. When the wooden deck below your bedroom window became wet and slippery and the little red flowers in the pots that you had hung out on the deck drooped and melted. When the streetlights shone in puddles on the deserted street and the water rose and fell as the raindrops pricked its surface. And the traffic piled up and people drove slowly and warnings went out on the radio. Did you think then, as I often do, of those endless showers of our only monsoon together, those long rain-logged lunches when we talked and bantered and fell in love?

It was my first job, my first trip on the Rajdhani express with its new chair cars, seventeen hours straight to Bombay Central. I was excited, the kind of excitement I cannot even pretend to feel these days. From that first day itself, Bombay hit me hard. Later I would learn that it was the typical manner of that strange, hateful, lovable, awful big city. It blew me off my feet with its richness, its freshness and something that my youthful fancy pinned down to a sense of freedom. Now I understand that freedom better: just a sense of extreme alienation that allowed people to live as immediate neighbours, in crumbling buildings whose faces were eaten raw by the salt of the sea, behind carved doors of walnut wood, and not feel obliged to know each other beyond a cursory greeting as they waited for the old lift to come down the well of the circular staircase. It allowed a clean, well-fed and well-dressed person to walk, with an easy conscience, past maimed children, lice infested, their tummies bloated, their eyes afloat as they languished on the roadside or on the metal bridges of the local rail stations. Naini should have seen those children; she would never feed her blasted Chihuahua again.

The first fifteen days, I stayed in a borrowed bed at the YMCA. My room-mate, Wakankar, must be a rich man now, too busy, too successful ever to feel as small and lost as I do now. He was a management trainee in a paint company but the share market was his real passion. In those fifteen days he went wrong only once on the share market. Each morning the *Economic Times* would scrape across the cement floor, bearing its message of profits and losses. By breakfast all the decisions would have been taken and the broker advised on what to sell and what to buy during the day. Then, that one hectic hour behind him, Wakankar would go through the day as if nothing mattered any more, his hands in his pockets, an old Mukesh tune on his lips. I admired and envied him; in fact, since then I have always admired and envied cool, nonchalant, decisive men.

I didn't share any of that nonchalance. The man whose bed I had borrowed was due to return from Goa in two days and I would be out in the cold again. I had followed every advertisement, every tip in the last two weeks. From Bandra to Colaba, on the seafronts of Marine Drive and Worli, I had been to countless old buildings with strong wooden doors and huge brass handles, but without success. All the rooms in the world seemed to have been already rented out or promised. And the few that were still available were too expensive for me.

I waited, hopes rising and falling like the fickle fortunes of the shares in which Wakankar dabbled. The eternal fantasy of being a paying guest of a kindly landlady with a pretty daughter in a room with a balcony on the sea dimmed with each passing day.

There had been only one moment of real hope—in a fourth-floor flat in one of the crusty, sea-facing buildings on Marine drive. The tall, old man who opened the door invited me into a room where his wife and daughter sat, in the dim light, sunk into enormous sofas, nursing their drinks. Sitting in that room, those three figures seemed to have emerged, for some obscure purpose, from a cubist painting, carrying with them their shadowy angularities. I felt that I had walked into a set scene, where the three of them had poured their drinks and had been waiting for me to take the left turn from Churchgate, walk down the road, come up the lift and ring the bell. As they started their questioning, they seemed to me like a wretched interview board, each trying to be smarter than the other, catty and polite.

'Do you know any of the directors on the board of your company?' asked the old man, his voice gruff with decades of smoking.

'What do you like to do in the evenings? I mean, do you like a lot of late nights?' said the wife, her sherry glass poised against her pearl necklace.

'What *I* would like to know,' the daughter paused dramatically as she threw a long arm over the sofa to scratch the powder puff of a dog on the carpet, 'is whether or not you play gin rummy.'

I didn't answer too well. With rising nausea, I wondered what on earth I was doing there. They were bored ghosts caught in some time warp. The dim light, the crystal glasses, the polished wood furniture and the three surreal figures made me claustrophobic. I excused myself and almost ran out, pausing only when I was down on the road by the sea, headed towards Churchgate station.

One evening, the last evening of Ganesh Chathurthi, I followed the crowd towards Chowpatty beach, as it pushed towards the dark, yawning sea. A slender white cloud, shaped like a long balloon, floated above the horizon and began to move towards the moon. On the beach the brightly decorated trucks and tractors and vans stood on the sand, their headlights carving out wide paths into the sea. People swarmed all around me, on the trucks, on the sand, in the water. Singing and dancing people, tired or sleepy or drunk people on the sand, down to the water. Each group brought with it its own statue of Ganapati to immerse into the sea. I followed four men who had picked up a statue and begun to wade into the water. The water was soon up to their waist, their shoulders, their necks. I saw their heads bobbing above the water, silhouetted against the light from the trucks. Then the statue lay horizontal and was pushed into the sea vigorously. It needed three duckings before it finally drowned into the water where it would dissolve, like thousands of others that night, slowly, to the accompaniment of chants of Ganapati Bapa Morya. I saw an enormous Ganapati, more than a hundred and fifty feet high. A crane had been brought to lift it from the platform on the truck and drop it into the water. A smaller statue, its pink phosphorous colours glinting in the headlights, was pushed on a set of rails into the water, like a ship being put to sea. Behind me, as I slowly began to walk away, light-headed and strangely calm in the clamour of a big city, the processions still clogged the streets, waiting for their chance to get to the water, to lay their own gods, gods of villages, colonies, townships, lanes to rest in the bottomless Arabian sea. The balloon of a cloud had almost reached the moon.

I wouldn't have found a room in Bombay if I hadn't found Chuck that night. He slapped me hard on the back as I walked away from the statues at the edge of the sea. I hadn't seen him in over three years, not since the days of the undergraduate hostel, where he was perpetually asleep in a small hot room in a white T-shirt and faded blue denim shorts. At night he would wake up to jump over the single brick wall of the swimming pool and do several lengths in the tepid water under the light of the moon. He had obviously done well judging from his neat shirt, black formal trousers, wire-rimmed spectacles and an air of quiet sophistication.

We found a table on the first floor of a crowded restaurant with high ceilings and old-fashioned fans that swung lazily from long rods. The waiter greeted Chuck with familiarity and as he wiped the table I noticed that he had six fingers. Then he swung the cloth back on his shoulder and was gone almost before Chuck had ordered 'two beers, strongwala.'

'Strong beer?'

'Yeah, it's something called Lager 200. Good stuff, double strength.'

We drank as the restaurant filled up with all sorts of people. People just hanging around, people going home from office, people meeting other people. I liked the fact that each table was a world of its own and people talked as if they were the only ones sitting in the place. It reminded me of the University coffeehouse and many half-forgotten conversations with Chuck. We talked of all sorts of things, going back and forth through the years.

Outside, the night was light and pleasant. Double-decker buses came swerving up to us and we jumped onto one as it took a wide turn around Flora Fountain. We sat on the upper deck. The bus was nearly empty at that time of the night, the air smelt of the sea and flowers.

'Join us in Sunshine Terrace. I'm sure Ducky won't mind a third. And we need the cash.'

'Sunshine Terrace?'

'Yes, Sunshine Terrace. Can you imagine it? Just think for a moment of the French Riviera. Sunshine on the terrace. Little tables with tall glasses. Coloured umbrellas. The spray of the surf and the smell of the sea. Occasional romances. Lazy and indifferent. Life at its most useless, indolent best.'

In the end it was as easy as that. Happily I felt the night close around us. At the beach the last of the statues were now being pushed out to the water's edge and soon the city would be asleep, shrouding for a few hours its million miserable little struggles.

I wonder if Sunshine Terrace is still there. It should have been pulled down years ago in the interests of safety and decency. But in those days, for Chuck and Ducky and I and for the other five hundred or so Bombayites who lived in its poky rooms on six floors around a huge hollow square, it was home.

To reach room F-16 on the sixth floor we had to go up the creaking flight of termite-ridden wooden stairs, taking care not to step on the weak parts. Then past rooms full of noisy children, harried mothers, blaring televisions, radio jingles and the smell of burnt cooking oil. Most of the excitement centred around the hollow square as the shouting, cheering children, some so small that they had to hold on to each other so as not to go over the railing, flung buckets on long ropes into the square. The buckets clanged and swung their way down to the filling team of elder brothers and sisters on the water tank below who joyfully poured mugs of precious water into the buckets. Then the fathers, sweating in their vests, would be called out to pull up the buckets. Each time a bucket sloshed over the railing, the children shouted and did a little victory dance, sticking out their tongues at the group across the square. It was as good a form of recreation as any and more innocent than most.

Once inside F-16, the world was shut out, forgotten. Deep conversations, tortured self-analysis, unsuccessful love lives took over. Ducky was the management guru and he taught us all that he had learnt from Peter Drucker who smiled approvingly from the bookshelf. Here, while water buckets swung and clanged outside, business empires were dreamt up. Power play was practised on corporate chessboards to which I brought my daily bit of input as the probationer working in the human resource division of a chain of five-star hotels.

There were only two beds and one sofa. A chart indicated the days on which each one of us would take a turn to sleep on the sofa in the half room, or the shit-end, as Ducky called it. The dreaded sofa night on poky, uneven springs could be avoided only under one condition written on the chart in green felt pen against a prominent asterisk:

*IF ANY OF THE INMATES RECEIVES A VISIT FROM A LADY FRIEND OF DECENT REPUTE, HE SHALL HAVE FIRST PRIORITY TO THE FULL BEDROOM. SUCH VISITS, BY COMMON CONSENT, SHOULD BE RESTRICTED TO TWO A MONTH.

I never had that privilege.

Friday evenings were guided by the Diceman. This was the arrangement we arrived at to sort out eternal differences about what to do. We would roll the dice and the man who got the highest count—the Diceman—would decide how the evening was to be spent and the others would have to agree. The Diceman decided whether we ate at the pure vegetarian Punjabi dhaba round the corner with its butter naans and dum aloo and shahi paneer or at the little Parsi place called Paradise that served pizzas and sandwiches and homemade fruity ice cream. On other nights the Diceman commanded us to walk into a moonlit sea until the water came up to our necks or take a taxi to the red-light area, pick up a fight and bring home a cheap whore or tell each other our most guilty secrets or confess the worst lies that we had ever spoken. The Diceman could not be denied.

It was neat and it was fun. But how could I have explained it all to Joy, craning over to read my e-mail from Rohini?

6

I never told Mina about you, Ro. I never told her though at times I wanted to. But I had decided a long time ago that I was not going to, that you were still too raw, too fresh a cut, to become a conversation piece. I don't know if you ever told your husband about me and if so then how much. If we were to meet, for instance, would he shake hands with me, welcome me into the house, share a drink with me, sit with us at the table and watch us exchanging glances, smiles and looks that held meaning only for us?

I could not bring myself to tell Mina about you and about your laughter that first attracted me to you in that room in Bandra on New Year's eve. You were surrounded by strangers, dark, smart men, seeking to enter the magical circle created by your laughter, so beautiful and free that it made each of them, and me, feel that in making you laugh we had realized all of life's delightful and careless vagrancy.

I stole you away in minutes from that crowd of journalists, advertising executives and young management trainees and we forgot them as they stood around a table crowded with beer bottles and plates piled high with potato wafers and an oval dish full of little mushroom vol-au-vents. We were only dimly aware, in our sudden complicity, of others who lounged on mattresses and cushions thrown in the corners, intense men chatting quietly to dark-eyed, long-haired women or the two couples who danced to the pounding rhythm of Funky Town.

With your back to the open window you dismissed with an imperious glance the man who had brought you to the party, the boy next door, fat five years ago, chubby still, who had recently got a good job, already defeated beyond hope because you obviously knew him too well to be attracted to him. You had probably played dark room, carrom board and cards as children during summer holidays and he had been considered a good safe chap to go swimming with or escort you to such parties. He would drop you back home in his second-hand car without having the guts to try anything on the way. You dismissed him and your laughing lips at last touched red wine. And as we danced you kept your long straight hair away from your face with gentle firm shakes of your head and you moved gracefully on the balls of your feet. Did I see it then, or did I imagine it in the swirling light—a shadow around your eyes, an occasional sudden seriousness that questioned your laughter and then vanished, lost. It gave you a mystery and it hooked me. As I threw myself into a chair next to you and drained half a bottle of beer, I was already in love.

I smile to myself at the thought of your laughter and I keep my face towards the window in this train. This smile is sacred; it is secret. It comes from warm places in my heart, from sunlit corners still not invaded by weariness, bitterness. I don't want to share it with anyone and I wait for it to fade, my inner glow to subside. We are beyond the rain now but the drops of water still cling to the window bars and the sunlight slants through the clouds in widening streams.

'Nothing in this world is perfect, not even your laughter.'

For a minute she was silent and gave me a deliberate, searching look. I returned the stare, playing the game.

'Wise guy?'

'Sort of.'

'That's a useful line, actually. About nothing being perfect . . . Perhaps I'll borrow it.'

'Please do, with my compliments. Dedicated to the mystery of your smile and the flashing spirit of your eyes.'

'You won't feel so great once you know how I'm going to use it. Nothing is perfect, not even your shoe polish . . . or something like that.'

'You write copy?'

'Literature. But for the moment I let it be sold as copy.'

'And when does it become literature?'

'When I get tired of calling some muddy, uninspiring nail polish 'coffee cloud'. As of today, I enjoy it.'

'I like you.'

'I like yoghurt.'

'Believe me, I'm not drunk. Will you see me tomorrow? Have lunch with me, have dinner with me, walk into the sea with me?'

'Tomorrow, smart guy, is next year. And I never think that

far ahead. Call me next year.'

In the morning I recalled her number through the mild, slightly sick headache that I have associated permanently with New Year's day. Her voice was clear, fresh, ready to go.

'Happy New Year.'

'Oh God!'

'As promised.'

'I thought you were part of that lousy old year and would have vanished with it.'

'Catch me.'

'I suppose you want to invite me out for dinner.'

'How did you guess?'

'I know your type. And the answer is no.'

'Hey come on.'

'But lunch suits me, if you can get out of bed that is, after all that beer.'

I threw away the sheet and sat up and nearly fell off. It was just my luck to be at the shit-end on New Year's day.

'I am out of bed.'

'Like hell.'

Rohini chose the place. A cafe attached to a theatre. I rarely went there because I felt odd in my formal clothes among the usual crowd that hung around there, drinking coffee between rehearsals, between careers, between marriages.

'It's not that I'm the arty type,' she said. 'It's just one of those few places where a girl can sit alone. Even a copywriter has a right to a few square feet of sunshine though she does ruin her chances by sharing it with guys on the make like you.'

'You don't look like the kind of person who would end up sitting alone anywhere.'

She wore a cream sweater and matching pleated trousers. A

wine-coloured scarf was knotted stylishly at her neck. As I watched her go through the menu, I saw again the hint of sadness around her eyes. But there was no sadness in her talk, only banter and laughter. My heart lifted just to hear her talk.

'I bet you I can get through this before they get the cold salad. You want to know everything about me. Don't deny it, I can see it on your face. You want to know what makes up this bewitching woman, the kind you have never met before—or so you'll tell me any minute now. Well here goes—Father, leading lawyer who gave me up for good when I told him that I would never wear the black coat; mother—died twelve years ago; one sister, one dog and a few cats. Profession—copywriter; ambition— to become a female novelist with long painted fingernails who gets photographed by *Time Magazine* against a tiger skin; Determination—negligible; favourite thing—hot jalebis with vanilla ice cream. That should do for a beginning. I function on a need-to-know basis, you see.'

'You have beaten the cold salad. I'm afraid I can't quite tell you about myself so quickly. Perhaps I am a bit complicated, comparatively speaking.'

'Oh God, he's not only persistent, he's complicated too.'

But soon I wanted to tell her everything. All the wild ideas that came to my head at night, fresh as the smell of rain outside my window. All the mistakes that I had made and all the bits of beauty that I had ever seen.

When that lunch was over, I wanted to see her again. Her mouth twisted in a reluctant pout, she agreed. And each time I met her I waited with a strange exciting anxiety for the moment when we would fix up our next meeting. In the restaurant amongst the cool green of the potted plants, on top of double-decker buses, on the steps of large open-air galleries. I had never talked so easily, laughed so openly with anyone. Rohini listened to me, and I found my personality being dissected by her, not antagonistically or sympathetically, but with a strange honest truthfulness. One Saturday afternoon we sat for a long time after lunch in a quiet old-world restaurant where nobody seemed to be in a hurry. The sun shone strongly outside. Old waiters in white canvas shoes and white cotton trousers and thin red ties hung around a piano in the shadows. On a paper napkin I scribbled—

I empty out my pocketful of daily doings
And you hold each one
Up against the sun.

She didn't say anything but screwed up her eyes in the peculiar way she had and put the napkin in the book she was carrying and, without laughing, kept the book in her bag. She did not say anything and our deal became clear to me. We were to care and not to show. We had to wrap up our love in banter and funny stories and if we hurt each other, it was not meant to matter. Enough people loved seriously, soberly. We weren't going to be lovers like that.

'Come on, tonight I'll show you my Bombay,' Rohini tugged at my elbow and started off down the pavement as soon as we came out of the movie hall. In her eyes there was a wild light. In her crisp walk there was a promise. She stepped lightly among the puddles of rainwater that reflected the red and green and yellow neon lights and I had to walk with extra long steps to keep up with her. We walked into a mela in the large oval.

The giant Ferris wheel rose up above the lights into the sky. I saw the dim stars far away and instinctively put my arm around her shoulder. As we reached the highest point of the circle and began to descend, she screamed and held her stomach. I pulled her towards me as the lights of the fair rose to meet us. Afterwards, we walked unsteadily around the fairground. Her eyes shone as she put a bottle of flavoured milk delicately to her lips and raised the bottle with uncomplicated, straightforward joy.

Suddenly she turned.

'Let's go and eat something. I'm famished. And tonight there's going to be none of your staid stuff. We'll eat what I want.'

What she wanted was pau bhaji at a crowded stall opposite the dimly lit Victoria terminus. The bhaji cooked with generous swathes of butter. The paus drenched in melted butter.

Then she turned to the next stall with four large earthen jars with garlands of marigold flowers around their necks. The jal jeera seared the throat and made our eyes water.

'What now?' I asked, racing along with her through the evening crowd, in the shadow of the old buildings with their spires and arches, through underground pedestrian tunnels with their white tiles and blue tube lights and onto Marine Drive and the dark sea beyond.

'Now we will ride in a Victoria. But first we will have paan.'

The paan was dipped in red sticky-sweet syrup and coconut shavings and melted in the mouth by the time we reached the Victoria standing at the traffic lights. It was a beautiful carriage with brass lamps and carved armrests pulled by a large black horse with golden tassles hanging from its ears. The traffic had eased and we rode at a fast clip past the weather-beaten buildings. Past the bandstand and the little beach with its refuse of cocunut shells and late-night merrymakers. Beyond the beach the road was suddenly empty. Except for something lying in the middle. The horse slowed down and then stopped.

'It's a body,' Rohini said, evenly, without emotion.

I jumped down. Rohini did not move.

I peered at the body. It suddenly gave an unmistakable sign of life—a loud snore.

'Damn it all, he's not dead. He's just drunk.'

I turned the man by the shoulder.

'Hey, I even know him. He's the guy who polishes shoes opposite Churchgate. Yesterday he polished my shoes. Imagine—in this big city! What a coincidence.'

But Rohini was not listening. She was sitting on the edge of the pavement now, her face pale, her trembling shoulders hunched over her knees, her fingers in her hair. I held her gently by her shoulders and she stood up, sobbing.

'It's all right,' I said, 'he's not dead.'

'But there are so many others who are dying all the time. I hate death. Let's get out of here.'

We climbed back into the Victoria and as the horse started moving again, she fell against my shoulder until her cheeks felt wet against my neck.

'I've been scared ever since Mama died. I was only ten. I saw her when they brought her back in the car from the hospital. I never want to see anyone dead again.'

I held her tight. Nobody who could laugh like her should have to cry. I would ensure that, forever. I bent down and kissed her wet cheeks. Then she threw her head back on the edge of the seat and let me kiss her lips while we rode to the point where the land vanished into the midnight sea.

7

After all these years, when all the edges have been worn out of my head, all the things that I hid from myself have been said, it is really quite simple to put down the truth. I betrayed Ro. I left her because my father refused to let me marry her—she was not of the right caste. And besides, he said as he looked at me intensely over his reading glasses, he knew all about her mother. A woman to whom that distracted man, Rohini's father, should never have got married. An actress of sorts, in those days—so what kind of family did I think she came from? She had died young because she used to drink too much. Finished her liver when she was not yet thirty-five. And of course all daughters ultimately end up doing what their mothers did.

I still do not know how my father found all that out. I never cared to ask him. I never want to bring up that moment when I caved in, when instead of standing up to him, I let him blackmail me with a mixture of anger and emotion. In the final analysis, I simply gave her up. There is a certain comfort in being able to understand this, in being able to say it out straight: when it mattered, I failed. Nothing had quite prepared me for the moment. Not the quaint liberal school, nor the sprawling University where I had read for long hours under the long fans descending from the library ceiling. Not the exhilarating midnight discussions on love and truth on the long walks among the thorny trees of the ridge around the campus under low moonlit clouds. None of this had managed to give my soul the courage of its conviction.

When I told her, she stared at her plate for a long time and then, in a tone which she would normally use to order another fresh lime and soda, she said:

'Marriage, whoever talked of marriage?'

Her face rose up like the chiselled face of some cold and lonesome heroine. Her eyes seemed to stare through me at some distant purple hills. I felt like I had been caught laughing in a room where somebody had just died. Behind her the sea was brutally blue in the sun, and the ships were still.

That evening Chuck was the Diceman and he was relentless. He looked at the ceiling. We would go to Marine Drive, he said, or to Chowpatty and we would get ourselves a real woman. The kind of woman whom we would want to sleep with, not the miserable creature we had got from the red-light area and released after paying her a hundred rupees like some child lets a parrot out of the cage after buying it and bringing it home. This would be different. And when we got her, it seemed like she had been waiting for us. Sitting on the sea wall, holding a fluttering blue-and-white saree with her left hand, eating a roasted bhutta with the other, a round bindi on her forehead, a fresh gajra of white flowers in the bun of her hair. She came without a word, with only one glance each at the three of us. The Diceman also decided the turns we would take. And when I entered her, she was still warm from Chuck, his sweat still clung to her neck, I could taste his cigarette on her lips. I added to her my frustration, my loss, my despair and my weakness. And then hating myself, finishing my half glass of neat rum in a gulp, I left the room and went running down the steps of Sunshine Terrace.

It was drizzling and the wet breeze from the sea began to stiffen and I liked it. It reminded me of the breeze that whistles through the pines in the hills. But here the silences and the solitudes of the hills were missing. Only the rush and the sweat and dirt and noise. I walked along the platform at Churchgate and boarded the train. I didn't know whether it was an express or a local and didn't care. As the train picked up sudden speed and then almost immediately began to slow down for the next station I pushed myself into a corner. I would get a seat soon but not by the window. A desperate foursome playing cards on a briefcase balanced on a pair of knees occupied those seats. They were squinting at the cards as if their lives were being foretold there. As if they could see in those cards when they would have their own house, when their children would find respectable jobs or get married, when finally they would die at the logical end of all these journeys. Maybe something that the cards told them would help them face their wives and kids back at home, in the squalid little apartments, give them a ray of hope on which they could sleep. It was all so important to them but it didn't matter a damn to anybody else.

I knew that I didn't matter to the next man engrossed in his newspaper. It wouldn't matter at all if I shook him and tore up his newspaper and told him all about myself, about Sunshine Terrace and my job, about the guilt and the anger, about Rohini and the pain that was trapped forever behind her careless laughter. I knew that each one of us is on his own, a prisoner, a lonely hero. I could see the whole world inside my head. That was where I would live. That was the where all the colours were; only their shadows fell outside.

My head began to swim as the train moved from station to station, through little tunnels and under crowded pedestrian bridges, past stinking backwaters and brightly lit highways. I moved to the window when the card players left. I felt light-hearted but something kept swirling up to my throat.

I felt free, free of Sunshine Terrace and the dim bulb that hung in our room, free of hope and of any need to love and be loved, free of so many things that my shoulders actually felt light. One could be free of anything if only one thought the right way.

The buildings swung lazily before my eyes. I wanted to be the boy who was having a careless bath under the street tap. I wanted to feel the thrill of the water flowing over my shoulders, washing away the whole wretched sweaty day.

The slum and high-rise blended with the night. The suburban stations all seemed alike with their glint of the bottles of cold milk and orangeade, the push and the shove. Two women were fighting on one platform, their sarees pulled up over their dark, knobby knees, their fish baskets flung aside. People walked past them. People walked past everything, their eyes blank and their minds far away. They walked the same places every day, they knew all the ways. They walked past Sunshine Terrace without knowing the world of clanging buckets inside. They walked past a boot polish boy not knowing that he had made a laughing girl cry all over again. They knew all the timings of the buses and the trains and even the fast trains. They knew that they were late if they did not see a particular face under a large hoarding which read 'Something wonderful coming your way . . .' All their endless humdrum days it was coming. It never would.

The rum swirled once again in my head, contradicting the clarity of my thoughts. Then I saw the girl in the corner, talking to a man. She seemed very far away. She looked so much like Rohini. In fact it must be Rohini, pretty and challenging, laughing and sad.

I got up and moved towards her.

Something caught my foot as I pushed towards her and I fell face forward. I clutched wildly for support and I think I brushed her arm.

'Drunk idiot.'

Something hard hit me on the head, twice. I fell back and something else hit me on the neck and then there was only the darkness.

When I came to, I felt a trickle of water on my face. A fresh, swishing sound poured down in the darkness around me. Rain from the night sky. It blew in great gusts from the sea and swept against the sides of the stationary train and the spray came in from the half-shut door. I knew that the half-shut door meant that the train was in for the night. Probably in Bombay Central.

I held the steel bar near my hand and stood up. The pain shot in arrows through my head and my hand could feel a soft and sticky mess on my neck. My jeans felt wet and I could smell vomit against the freshness of the rain. I had to get home.

I stumbled over the rails, feeling the strength return gradually to my legs. A hammer in my head kept time with my steps. I walked past the silent long trains sleeping in straight lines like monster caterpillars preparing for an invasion. In a few hours they would rise as if in response to a bugle call and feed life into a cavernous, helpless city. Hundreds of thousands of faceless pieces of life would be picked up and thrown in relentlessly, along with their sweaty breath and their little slimy claws. Some would fall off or get electrocuted as they rode on the roof of the trains; others would merely have their pockets picked but there would be no letting up, no stopping for breath.

On the platform, the sleeping bodies did not move as I walked past them. A woman, obviously insane, took off her shirt and, naked under the yellow light, laughed. The shrieking laughter went through my heart.

The Irani teashop outside the station was open. Some of the tables still had chairs lying upside down on them. I found a table that had been straightened and wiped clean. The slot games had been switched on and from one of them a pink and blue Dolly Parton winked at me. The owner sat at the counter, half-hidden by the glass jars of orange sweets and shiny chocolates. He was reading the newspaper of the day before. He shouted into the curtain behind him for the tea and went back to the newspaper without a second glance. When the tea came, it was hot and sweet and as I took a sip I smiled. Nothing mattered. Nothing would from now on. In a couple of hours, it would be dawn and then I would find a way, once and for all, to leave that city behind.

I have never been able to go to Bombay again, even on work, even when Basu offered, his right hand tickling his balls through his pocket, to take me along for a conference with a client company. I haven't been able to get over it. The sun shining on that blue sea will still break my heart, like I broke Ro's heart then, when the ships that stood out in the sea seemed to have been painted on a timeless canvas.

ROORKEE

1

There is a loud noise, a thud and a squeal. I jerk awake from an uneasy nap. Some cow across the line, perhaps. Or a boulder that could have derailed us and mercifully finished it all forever. Or maybe, since my life seems to be running like a film anyway, it is an armed robbery at midday by dacoits on white horses with huge turbans, double-barreled guns, curled moustaches and bloodshot eyes who will kill us all and take away the women and the gold and then come back and surrender to some honest police officer.

But it is only the faraway crack of lightning that has woken me up, a jagged bolt that pierced my cloak of sleep, for some reason sounding louder than it really was.

I turn to try and go back to sleep again, to see if I can stay lost in my corner for another half hour, just enough for the train to start slowing down for Roorkee. I like dozing off like this, turning my face away from the world, going back into darkness. And I look forward to the dreams that come, long or short, pleasant or suffused with want, dreams that leave me aching inside.

One of those evenings after Mina left, I dozed on the armchair out on the veranda, my unfinished drink by my side, a pink haziness in my head and dreamt of sex after a long time. A dream like the dreams one has when one is young, the kind of dream you wish would never end, a dream that haunts you for years and can give you a wonderful warm feeling just to think of it. It must have been the gin. Gin goes with sex like no other drink. Beer is too quick and whisky and brandy are too serious. Gin goes with sex only as jazz does. It has the same dragging quality, the lingering touch that lasts longer and leaves a better aftertaste. When I think of gin, I think of wide-open glasses with olives and club rooms with lazy barmen shuffling behind heavy bamboo curtains. And I think of lingering sweaty lovemaking on hot summer afternoons, of drugged sleep afterwards, of a pleasantly heavy head in the evening.

It was Rohini again, this time with dark lavender-flavoured skin. I found myself in a strange hotel with broad balconies and well-lit rooms. I was begging her, beseeching her to talk to me, and telling her that I had not talked to anyone for six months. And then I was undressing her, tentatively, compulsively, my heart throbbing like it throbs when it is our first time, waiting for her to tell me to stop, to put her hand out and push me away, to get up from the bed and run away sobbing and cursing. But she didn't stop me; instead she watched, smiling indulgently at me all the time. And then she lay back to enjoy my kisses. Behind her tousled head I saw someone through the window coming to my door and checking to see if it was open. Fortunately it was locked. I can recall its rosewood solidness like that of the huge beds of my parents' marriage, the beds that vanished somewhere without a trace. Whoever it was went away; a dark silhouette passed quickly against the faintly lit window. I turned back to her lavender-flavoured skin.

And then I woke up, with the feeling of sex uppermost in my mind and a sweet familiar yearning in every pore of my body. Outside it was raining, heavily, darkly and I closed my eyes again.

But the dream had vanished, only its intense image had settled down into the corners of my consciousness. Holding on to it like precious gold dust I went back to my half-finished drink.

Why do I dream of her so often? And I do not forget the dreams the instant I wake up. I carry them around with me for a long time. Once I dreamt of her wandering around in a strange house, a house with a big back veranda and a round rose garden and the heavenly fragrance of the night flowers from a huge bush just outside the window. She wore a blue-and-white checked cotton shirt and her hair fell in waves on her shoulders. I struggled with a hundred schemes to spend more time with her and take her away and make love to her. And once I dreamt I watched her from the back seat of her car, as she sat beside her husband, returning from a romantic birthday dinner just for two, the wedding band glittering on her finger.

The lightning crackles again. It seems nearer this time. There was lightning on the night I was born, my mother has told me several times. And there was rain. For a while people had thought that there would even be snow. But there was only the rain and later there was a white frost on the wheat fields and on the barren branches of the trees and lawns of my grandfather's government bungalow. That night the lightning scared my mother as she waited for the doctor in the dark labour room on the fifth floor of the hospital. The lights had gone out, blown away by the bluster of the wind and rain that howled victoriously through the open doors. It swept up the curtains and banged the windows until people pulled at the panes and latched them down and even then they creaked and groaned to be free. No candle, no lamp, no flame could stand up to that wind; the doctor delivered me by the instinct that several hundred deliveries had given to her hands. And then smiling and patting my mother on the cheek with her cold hands she was gone, down the five floors in the dark, wrapped up against the wind in a huge black shawl. The lightning continued to crack all night, my mother told me, and I cried through it all, my eyes squeezed shut tightly, dressed in a light blue cotswool frock on which navy blue cherubim rode jauntily on brooms, covered in thick hand-woven woollen sheets and cradled in the folds of the overflowing waist of my mother's grandmother.

That was how life began, hiding from lightning, in the dark. And that is how it is going on, my eyes squeezed shut from all that has been or will be, on a train between two nondescript towns, the lightning threatening me from across the fields of ripe sugarcane.

2

Rohini's e-mails, random signposts in barren, brown stretches, gradually began to fill up the years I had put behind me as best as I could. Each message carried a tiny secret of time, a hidden moment or a few years scratched into three short paragraphs, without capitals, hardly any punctuation marks, as if it was all so simple and inconsequential that it didn't even require the lifting of an extra finger. Quickly written e-mails as if she knew that if she stopped to think and analyse, if she paused to check her spelling, she may not send the message at all.

I searched in those messages for her story and got sometimes a full chapter, sometimes only a fragment, often just a hint. The lost years broke up into little packages, each travelling by a different route, following different stars. But somewhere it all began to add up and I began again to share with her the world that I had thought lost forever, sacrificed at the altar of compromise.

. . . there is so much to tell you that i don't know where to start. i am not even sure that you want to know. anyway it is only on e-mail. you can just delete it and nobody will ever find the scraps—you won't need any hidden dustbins or desperate secret bonfires of letters on the terrace . . . i met gautum in 1989. yes it wasn't all that long ago. i was alone for many years after bombay. i don't know if you ever knew. i don't think so. you probably thought that I left bombay and got married as soon as I could, didn't you? Well as usual you were wrong . . .

. . . in the beginning it was quite good, exciting and new and not too much of a mistake. a house in the suburbs, five minutes' drive from the metro station, three minutes to the supermarket, a good neighbourhood school if we ever needed one. gautum had planned it all; he was always good at planning! he researched it all, analysed it, discussed it. i let him handle it all, i wanted only to study and worried about admissions, financial aid, credits, day and night . . .

. . . here was my big chance to study in an american university, with majors and minors and libraries and computers and exciting new methods. it wasn't easy, it took me six months to apply, to get recommendations from bombay university teachers in sealed envelopes—they had probably forgotten me by then. finally I was doing it—a doctorate in english literature, a useless sort of doctorate . . .

Not useless, Ro, I wanted to tell her. But beautiful. To have the opportunity, the luxury of doing what one wants, to do it without guilt or pain—what else could one want? I wanted to tell her that I was happy that she got the chance; I was happy she took it.

> *. . . i mean useless because it wasn't business or finance or law. it wouldn't get me a job at the world bank or at the un or in some big company . . .*
>
> *for months i slogged it out. spending my afternoons and evenings at the university, saturday mornings at the library, nights reading late. gautum was always busy with his work. he travelled a lot, to london and mexico or to the west coast. sometimes he asked me to go with him, to use up all the frequent flier miles that he collected. but he would always be busy so i would let him go alone and i enjoyed it when he came back. in those days he would sit down and tell me about his trip, day by day . . .*

I read each message several times, searching for traces of anger, bitterness, hidden innuendo. I would read them after Joy left for the day, pointedly switching off her light and telling me that it was six thirty, already half an hour extra. As if she had anything better to do at home than cook the evening meal and eat it with her old mother. Then she would no doubt do one of those five ways things—wash her hair, colour her eyes or whatever. That time was the best—when she would leave, the light in my room would turn a warm yellow, the trees of Connaught Place below my window would turn into a darkening mass, frayed slightly at their edges, and the office would actually seem friendly.

Some of those messages were easy to read. And others, especially those that spoke of sharing things, time, space with her husband, I could not read fully. Some I understood instantly and associations gone faint began to bloom again. And others I understood only late at night, when the drink had gone home and opened up the dark uneven spaces of the heart. Often I felt that she was not telling me everything, that she was stopping short.

She was not telling me, for instance, that she missed Gautum when he was travelling, that she felt alone in her bed at night without him, that she waited for his call and talked about meaningless little things across oceans, that when he finally came back, she made love to him, hungrily, eagerly, fiercely. She did not tell me these things because she did not want to hurt me.

I too have changed, Ro. Such things do not hurt me any longer, but any attempt to hide them does. I do not need any protection any more. All I need is the truth.

I missed those messages when they did not come; I found myself making excuses for their absence. I would pace my office room until Joy would begin to wonder what was wrong. I knew I should not be behaving that way, like some teenage lover waiting at a bus stop for an afternoon tryst. I mean, if you started from the basics, the messages were not supposed to be there in the first place. Ro had long gone out of my life when we said goodbye and I walked off in the post-lunch sunshine beside the sea wall, when the painted ships stood still on the waters. There had been no promises of ever coming back into my life, of saving my sanity. The messages that came now out of the big blue so many years later were only a big bonus, a heavenly intervention, just one of those things. I could not depend on them—I had once depended on her laughter and I had not had the courage to keep her laughing. I could not get into that position—all the wisdom and the experience of my age, of my great, millennium-coinciding forty years, was against it.

Balls.

The battle was lost before it had begun.

3

Through the weeks of my own confusion and loss, I searched for hints in her e-mails and wondered what drove her away from Gautum and the peaceful, leafy, suburban life with its villas and backyards and barbecues, its mounds of brown dead leaves, its manicured lawns.

Was he a nice husband or just a tolerable one? Was there a spark in their marriage or was it just one of those things made on a short holiday in Delhi, in Ashoka Hotel, with the wilting garlands and melting Cassata ice cream? And then carried across the Atlantic, with the cultural baggage all checked-in—the calendar of festivals, the Indian music CDs, agarbatti, paan masala, basmati rice—to a land of blue jeans and green cards, of grim competition and tired success.

Did he help her clean up after dinner in that land of no servants or did he walk up to his bed, nightcap in one hand, the weekend newspaper in the other? Did they hold each other every night or only for the first three months? Did they move into separate beds after that, or even into separate bedrooms?

If only she would write more often and long, I wished, long as those conversations when we used to watch the sun sink into the sea, sipping tea in a revolving restaurant or walking home, dragging our steps.

One day she read my thoughts.

> *. . . how does one get up and just leave? leave a running house, cupboards full of our clothes, saturday mornings spent in pulling out winter things, putting away the summer whites, sundays spent in organizing the basement, tending the plants, making sure they didn't catch the frost . . . you*

*know all this sort of thing is difficult to just walk away
from. so i stayed on and on . . .*

She should have taken a course from Mina. Three quick ways to
painlessly leave your husband. No previous experience required.
All one needed, she would have discovered, was a friend like
Naini and a lover like Rajiv.

Joy once asked me whether I was into Iyengar yoga. She was
not probing, she was not acting smart. She was simply being
concerned and, I suspect, despite herself she was being a bit
corporate. In my early years with the company, I remember
reading a book that compared working for a company to living
in an ice palace where you pretty much did what the big bosses
did and if you were really good, you did it before them. I wasn't
too good at that sort of thing ever, which is why I did not catch
on to Iyengar yoga before Joy. I should have guessed she got the
signal from Angela, Basu's secretary, who of course got it from
Basu himself. After his laughing club thing he had discovered
Iyengar yoga. More likely, dear Neeta had got on to it and told
him what a great thing it was, how it helped her bind her day,
be in touch with herself all through it, helped her cleanse her soul
each evening and refresh her mental and spiritual capabilities. Or
some trash along those lines.

'Not really, Joy,' I told her, 'the few times that I have tried
to meditate, I have fallen asleep. And what I couldn't figure out
was why my teacher, or preceptor as he preferred to call himself,
who was telling me to concentrate on a single point of light,
could not make out the difference. Didn't say much for his
perception. In fact, he kept telling me that I was very spiritually
inclined and hence could get into a trance faster. Little did he
know that this comes from knowing how to stand and sleep in
DTC buses for a quarter of a century.'

What I didn't tell Joy is that I have my own trick, my secret equivalent of hours of Iyengar yoga. I can concentrate when I want. I can put the two fingers of each hand to my temples and think so hard about a place or time that it begins to live inside my head. I can feel the light, the sounds, the smells and when I am finished I collapse, tired with the effort. I used to do it a lot in college but now I let it be. I use the trick only when I can no longer help it.

When Rohini's e-mails hesitated, I fell back on the trick. With the office lights off, with Joy gone home to her mother, with Basu already into his second drink at the Habitat bar, I would put the two fingers of each hand on my temples and concentrate on Ro's life and what she had lived through and what she had left and why. My trick would fill up the gaps that her messages left.

I knew her house by now. A two-storeyed red brick house in a silent, out of the way street, a street with no outlet, a lightly uphill street with big trees and the perpetual sound of cicadas in the branches.

> . . . the house is rather nice. a large living room. I have done it up in black—leather sofas, high black lamps. There are red and brown rugs on the wall supposedly from turkey but to be honest bought from the Georgetown flea market. the living room opens onto a square deck which is nice in the summers, the guests like to sit out there and beyond the deck there is the rather small triangular yard with ancient trees and then only the large dog field . . .

I could imagine those balmy summer evenings. Wrought iron tables, sea-green citronella candles in large glass cups to match the glasses with thin stems in which dear Gautum must have splashed his second-rate Californian red wine and the guests would have smiled and argued and thanked Rohini at least twice before they left. All sorts of guests—World Bank economists, artists, photographers, lawyers, a collection of people, some genuinely interesting and some who Gautum no doubt thought would be useful sometimes.

Dog owners in swanky cars and SUVs brought their beloved Labradors, Alsatians and terriers to the dog field beyond their house, I suppose. Maybe Ro and Gautum too had a dog; she never mentioned one. Walks in the golden summer light along the trails that wound through the trees that surrounded the field, tennis at the community court, a yard sale every year, shopping for a dish antenna, a home gym, finally a home security system. Many afternoons at the mall, fighting the crowds at Thanksgiving, Halloween and Christmas. Or just on ordinary weekends, snipping coupons from the newspapers, looking for cheaper apples and onions, Indian groceries at the India store, barbeque equipment in the summer, gardening equipment in spring, snow cleaning stuff in the winter. Gautum mowing the lawn on Saturday mornings in summer in his shorts and T-shirt, grumpy and reluctant. She planting bulbs and flowers and taking out the weeds, a tune on her lips, gardening gloves on her hands, trying to time her work so as to take advantage of the rain and save on the water bills.

The whole picture makes me want to be sick. It probably wasn't true, but then, I wonder, could it have been much different?

4

On a day when even the messages did not still the mess inside me, when even the trick did not seem to work, I did something entirely shameful. It was as near as I could have been to visiting a whore or entering some smoke-filled striptease place with golden cages and powdered, sequined women. I went walking on Janpath to watch the girls. Suddenly I felt the need to feel the urge for a young woman again, to undress slowly with my eyes some innocent beauty as she walked indifferently past me. But when I reached Janpath I found that my eye had turned yellow— I didn't yearn for what I saw: the young, fresh women with their summer blouses that showed their arms and their shoulders and their rising breasts; women with hair tied up in clean knots to prevent the stickiness on the neck, necks with clean young lines and faint down and little moles. I watched them closely, clinically, in the beady fashion of a truly dirty old or at least middle-aged man. But I did not yearn. Once or twice I even stopped, stood aside near the shops and just watched them go by, humming a song, laughing carelessly, immersed in chatter. It was beautiful and strange and not at all sad. I wafted along with them, happy for them, hoping that their beauty and their youth and their laughter would fill that street for ever.

When I came back to office I could feel a warm glow on my cheeks. Panditji thought he had guessed the reason.

'Good paan this man at the corner makes. Genuine tambaaku, lasts at least an hour, hour and a half.'

I felt sad for him. He could not even imagine the far end of the mind, the dark terrain where I increasingly lived. I nodded, shut my eyes as if in ecstasy, puckered my lips pretending to spew out a straight line of red paan juice in his old but clean lift, saw his horrified anticipation and then, mercifully for him, got off at the third-floor landing. I felt guilty later. I shouldn't have done that. None of it was Panditji's fault.

5

I have said this before—I never told Mina about Ro. I never felt that I could tell her without my voice breaking, never felt that she would understand it the right way. But I did tell Ro about the time I met Mina and agreed to get married to her. I posted her a letter. I don't remember what I actually wrote. But Ro knows; she kept that letter, written on an off-white sheet and sent in a matching envelope. She kept it in a leather folder all these years, an old leather folder with cracks, I suppose, into which dust must have settled permanently. She kept that note; she did not tear it into tiny shreds in anger and bitterness. Somewhere she understood my weakness and forgave it. And now, so many years later, she sent my note back to me in an e-mail. This is the kind of thing I could never manage with Mina.

> . . . I met Mina recently, through some common friends of my father. Everybody is now insisting that it is time I got married. Papa had a heart attack in the summer and is rather weak so I really see no reason, frankly speaking, why I should continue to object to getting married though I must say that I am not too excited about all this. It was to please him after all that I did what I did. Mina is in a management course that she finishes in June and we are to be married a week later—her birthday, June 11. I am sending you the card, though I know that you are not likely to come ten thousand miles simply to attend this wedding. But I think I do need to tell you, I owe you that, I owe you much much more. I wish someday you would be able to remember me the right way.

For her part, she hadn't even sent that sort of note about Gautum, not even the obligatory two-weeks-before-the-wedding announcement to all earlier friends and lovers. Not until now, when she started sending me e-mails, making up for lost time, did I find out how she really met him.

> *i took the train and travelled to new york to see picasso at the met. those days i did things like that. from the fabulous union station to the dark underground penn station, new york, with a book of poems and a bottle of water to see me through those three hours as the train went through forest and across wide river mouths of the susqehanna and the deleware. those mysterious names always reminded me of campfires and laughing maidens and canoes in the rapids. i remember the small towns with desolate strip malls and huge car lots on the way, the windy golf courses and little houses with kitchen gardens near the railway line, the college girls in thigh-length leather jackets and blue jeans leaning against public call booths, a bunch of road workers in bright green and orange vests leaning for a moment on their shovels and brooms to exchange gossip, an abandoned rail track curving away into a clump of trees . . .*
>
> *i ran up the escalator at penn. the city was already making me walk faster. i didn't want to take a taxi or a bus and decided to walk. i walked like new yorkers do, just crossing the streets forward or sideways, depending on which light is green, knowing everything was at right angles and i would never get lost . . .*

I stared at my computer screen, struggling to evoke the picture. Fitfully I succeeded, beads of perspiration already forming under the fingertips pressed into my temples. I could imagine her running up the escalator to the street level at Penn station, her backpack bouncing lightly on her shoulders. She walked fast and proud, her stride stretching as she crisscrossed to Broadway and waited for a moment at Times square, taking in its gigantic advertisements and its famous names. On her right she could see the Empire State Building rising into the clouds, the sun reflecting on the discs and metal poles near the top. A bit further on was the shining steel top of the Chrysler building with its arched roaring tigers. She walked fast, at times moving faster than the buses in the traffic, past pizza shops, Chinese dry-cleaners, discount stores, fancy boutiques, the homeless man stretched out, still asleep at midday, oblivious of the crowd and the noise, one arm flung out, palm facing the narrow strip of sky. Snatches of Russian, Polish, Greek, clipped English accents swished past her. The shop windows reflecting the busy street: the shoppers and the tourists, the middle-aged executive with his spring coat thrown loosely over his shoulder, continuously running his fingers through his thinning hair as he walked, the girl in the tight leather skirt, smoking in style she sauntered across the street, the elegant lady in a camel wool coat, walking the dog near her apartment building just beyond the awning of the porch where a guard stood in a brown uniform, his soft cap in his hand, nodding in response to a garrulous cabbie.

> ... i stared at the blue paintings. they reflected the mediterranean in all its serene and cultured beauty and ancient confidence. surprisingly there were very few people in the halls that day. i could sit on the bench in the centre of the room and take it all in. only one man stood in front of the blue painting of a man in a hat. every few minutes he would change his position and walk across and look at the

*painting from another angle. it disturbed me a lot. i got up
to tell him that if he really didn't mind could he try to
remember that there were others in the same room who were
trying to see the same painting. but as i went up to him i
heard him talking to himself. he was demented i thought—
one of those lunatics who went around destroying precious
pieces of art—slashing, spraying, stealing. then he had
turned and i looked into his eyes. they were kind and gentle,
not the eyes of a man who would slash a beautiful
painting . . .*

With jealousy clasping my throat, I heard their dialogue from the
past being replayed in front of me:

'You are Indian,' she blurted out in surprise.

'And so are you,' he spoke in his nice and gruff voice.
'Doesn't surprise me at least. One in every six people in the world
is an Indian.'

She was quiet.

'I love this painting,' he said, not wanting to end the
conversation.

'It is one of the most beautiful of this period. I've been
staring at it from the bench there.'

They stood for a while and talked about the paintings.
Almost unconsciously they moved together to the next room.
Rohini felt a comfort in his presence, comfort that assured her
that he would not take it amiss that she was walking along with
him. So when he shyly offered her 'a coffee or something'
standing in the cathedral-like lobby of the museum, she accepted.
Beyond the heavy wooden doors the day had changed dramatically.
Clouds darkened the late afternoon and the sky scrapers were now
sombre and distant. A strong cold wind was blowing, funnelled

by the narrow corridors of the tall buildings and as they crossed the street, cold big raindrops began to fall.

'Let's hurry,' Gautum said, looking up at the sky. 'I know a place not very far away.'

He walked fast and she had to take a few running steps every few yards to keep up with him.

'Sorry, I walk too fast,' he said, slowing down, 'just one of those bad habits.'

'It's not a bad habit,' she replied and he turned to smile at her. He had a gentle smile that seemed to start in his eyes and spread across his face like a good-natured glow.

'I thought you were some mad man out to slash through that Picasso,' she said, with a half-embarrassed smile. 'In fact I thought you were even talking to yourself.'

'I was.'

'What?'

'Yeah, I was just telling myself, New York, the Met, Picasso— lucky swine, you are here.'

He held the door open for her when they reached the teashop. It was crowded with people moving in from the rain.

'Let's go to the back if we can get a table. It's quieter in there.'

She followed him past the long counter loaded with pastries, muffins and doughnuts, past the baskets of freshly baked breads, polished red and green apples. They got a small table for two at the back of the teashop. Through the low window they could see the lights of New York reflected in the puddles, disturbed only by hurrying footsteps.

That was how Rohini and Gautum got to know each other, over two pots of Darjeeling tea and a basket full of fresh raisin bread.

6

Just stay in the present, just watch the fields go by beyond this train window. Wait for the eucalyptus trees that line the hundred-and-fifty-year-old Ganga canal to come up on the horizon. Then I will know that I am reaching Roorkee. Cling on to the present. The past is too far gone. Too much has happened since, we are all too old to think of those things, things that happened when we were only children. Bright, true, believing, freshly cut, so fresh that it still hurts. If one goes back into the past, one would want to undo so much. It would make me go insane and then Mina and Basu and all the others who think like them will be able to smile smugly.

I should take a hint from Ro's e-mails. She tries, for the most part, not to mention those Bombay days, almost as if our deal of silence can be revived, almost as if we can reignite our different kind of love.

I wonder, how long do these things stay, how much can the bonds of youth be stretched? Those few innocent months in Bombay are worth more to me than the vast spread of years since. I stayed with Mina for fourteen years, slept with her so many nights, fought with her, screamed at her, then, limply, allowed her to dump me and walk off with another man. Almost half a life together, and yet I was never as close to her as I had been to Rohini. Those few youthful kisses were worth all the rest.

The chalk-white slender trunks of the eucalyptus shine in the distance. They are the only trees that break the open field. This canal is an old engineering feat, constructed to bring water to open plains, not a canal thick with brush and undergrowth and fallen trees, not like the canal that Rohini and Gautum walked along on their last morning together.

7

The C&O canal that she described lay in the shadow of its steep bank; the sun glinted through the trees and off the river that flowed alongside. Between the canal and the river were the silent trees, touched by spring, waiting for the bright summer. A few early cherry blossoms broke the green. Soon the entire place would burst into lush beauty. The dappled sunlight floated on the walking path. Two cyclists talked to each other as they strained on an uphill stretch; their voices carried unnaturally loud in the silence. A squirrel carried a bushy baby in its mouth as she climbed the thin upper branches of a birch until she could go no further. A lone runner was jogging in front of them, a Labrador running joyfully by his side. Two girls experimented with their cameras in this paradise of light and shade. Beyond the abandoned old lock of the canal was a bench, in a green alcove. They sat on that bench, in silence. I wondered until, gradually and in bits and pieces, she told me how they reached there.

> *sometimes i think back now and wonder what life would have been like if i had not left gautum and come away. or if i had left him much earlier, when i first felt the emptiness that became so permanent later. i suppose it is no use thinking of all these things. it will change nothing, neither the present that we have, nor the past that we have lost . . .*
> *i just got used to it all i suppose—got used to a lot of things . . .*

Year after year, I am sure, she had watched the seasons change, the grass grow and the leaves redden outside her bedroom window and then fall, scattering in yellow-brown bunches in the front and back yards and on the sloping roof until they blocked the drains and everybody got used to the brown messiness and nobody bothered any more.

She got used to the years coming to an end, one after the other. To the wonderful October light, to the ritual of Halloween costumes, the feasting at Christmas. Even to the sense of renewal at the end of every year, the hope hidden in the sadness of passing.

On that fall morning that she wrote to me about (or I imagined it, maybe) the fog was so heavy that she could not see the big trees outside her window. She liked to look at those trees first thing every morning. Sometimes in the spring, she would see a new burst of green or, in the summer, little red birds and black squirrels, poised on a twig, their bodies taut and expectant. In the winter she would see, through the bare pointed branches, the white barrenness of the field beyond. Beyond that field there were houses and lanes and once in a while she could see the top of a car or, at night, the wave of flashing headlights. She did not know anybody who lived in those houses; they seemed to be houses at the edge of the world. But she had seen white smoke rising from chimneys into a sky only a shade darker.

But that morning the fog was so thick, only a faint impression like smudged fingerprints indicated the presence of thick tree trunks. She sat on the sofa near the window, her legs curled under her, her red-and-black Naga shawl thrown loosely over her shoulders. She sat like that many mornings trying to summon up the energy to go out or to switch on the computer and download her e-mails or search the net for announcements or advertisements. She would sit there and read the two newspapers, drift through their indifferent sections, the local news, the style and fashion snippets or the political gossip that she could not relate to even after so many years. Or there would be her books, taken three weeks at a time from the public library. Mostly new fiction by women writers. Dense three-generation family sagas; or tales based on letters about a grandmother who had fallen in love with an oriental charmer; or travel books written by lonely women who had spent a year in France or Italy or Spain. Sometimes she too thought that she should write something, a book, perhaps her own story. Perhaps that would give her life a centre, something to look forward to when she got up in the morning, to think about as she lay sleepless in the long nights and watched the moon sink slowly over the field beyond the trees.

That day she left the newspapers untouched on the driveway. She would pick them up later, she told herself. Perhaps by then she may also summon up some enthusiasm to rake in the dead leaves on the front lawn. Any day now, she thought, the county truck would come to suck them up, crush them. The men in the truck would want them all neatly piled up next to the sidewalk on the road, neat little piles scattered only when children from the town houses across the road took flying leaps into them. Or she would need to mulch them and bag them. This happened every fall; and fall came every year. There was nothing more eloquent than piles of dead leaves to show the relentless passage of time. With a tremendous physical effort, she pushed herself away from the window and went downstairs to the kitchen to make a strong cup of coffee.

There had been a time when she wouldn't have dreamt of making a cup of coffee for herself alone. Coffee on the weekends had been a precious ritual between her and Gautum. He had been enthusiastic about coffee once, spending hours in front of the grinding machine in the supermarket, picking the beans, mixing them to get the right weight and aroma, grinding them appropriately fine for their kitchen percolator and bagging some separately for his office. He would make the coffee for both of them on Saturday mornings and pour it out on the back deck, adding the milk slowly over the back of a spoon. And they would chat and have two cups each, while the music floated from the study window, onto the deck and into the trees beyond.

She thought with a sigh that they had not had a Saturday morning like that for a very long time now. It was not as if Gautum had stopped drinking coffee. In fact he practically lived on it. Paper cups were always strewn around his office, along with Diet Coke cans and half-eaten pretzel packets. A smell of stale coffee clouded over the desperate days and nights that he and his colleagues spent there obsessed by a desire to see their company go public. It was now or never in the here today, useless tomorrow world of software technology. If somebody else got their idea off the ground before they did, years of work would go waste. But if they managed it first, all those days and nights, all those cups of coffee in the office would have been worth it. The company would go public, the shares would skyrocket on the stock exchange and Gautum would achieve his dream: not wealth—for he did not seek wealth—but financial security. He explained it to her several times, on foolscap sheets of white paper with graphs and calculations and equations, and handwriting that had begun to slope backwards. Methodically, he calculated for her how much money they needed. To keep that house, pay off all the mortgages, put any eventual children through college, get that second car. And never have to worry about the future. For the last five years now, she had watched Gautum chase that dream so hard that he had begun to live it. In the last argument that they had on the subject she had decided to confront him.

'We don't need financial security, Gautum. We are fine and the savings we have will see us through our old age even if we were to retire today. There are only two of us.'

He had looked up at her quickly and she had looked away. He knew there were only two of them. After two early miscarriages, she had never been able to conceive again.

She had decided then that there would be no more arguments. She would let Gautum chase his dream. She understood that ultimately his chase was not for security or for the comfort of vacations and freedom from mortgages. It was simply a desire to be up there with the rest of his classmates who had made it into the small group of millionaires from India. He too wanted to be interviewed in community newspapers, to be invited to embassy functions, be presented to the visiting Prime Minister as one who had achieved the great American dream and brought glory to his country in the bargain. It was his dream, she knew, that was invading their present.

As she sipped the coffee, she wandered aimlessly around the house. From room to room, as if seeing some of the things for the first time. There were parts of the house that they hadn't used for months. Like the alcove in the smaller part of the drawing room, with the green and blue chairs and the heavy walnut-wood chest of drawers. There were photographs on the wall above that chest of drawers. Photographs, from another lifetime, it seemed, of adventurous vacations, long drives to islands and mountains, even a seven-day drive from the east coast to the west through a vast empty landscape on a telescoping highway. In those photographs, Gautum was careless, glamorous, sporty. An outdoor man in a parka and cap, jaunty scarves around his neck, skiing down a slope, stepping into a canoe ... She was laughing in all those photographs. Careless and young.

She glanced into the antique mirror on the other wall. Her eyes said it all. Troubled and tired. With a fine network of lines that had begun to show at the corners. She stretched her neck to see if the crease there vanished. Not completely. She measured between her thumb and forefinger the wave of gray hair that led off from the centre of her head.

There hadn't been any vacation for the last three years. She recalled only travelling alone, to India for three weeks and once to Paris. Four days she had walked alone in Paris and done all the usual things. Gone up the Eiffel and stared down at the lazy Seine with its white tourist boats and ice-cream cafes under the bridges. Sat in the wayside cafes, rummaged through second-hand bookshops near the Notre Dame, listened to music in the streets and exhausted herself in the labyrinthine corridors of the Louvre. She had pored over her guidebook and walked the streets with the famous names. But when she came back home, there were no shared moments to savour, no remembered cadences from the music and nobody to tug at the elbow and remind how the light had filtered through the stormy clouds over Paris and glinted off its gilded domes.

She started violently at the ringing of the telephone, almost as if someone had shaken her by the shoulder. The three instruments—in the bedroom, the kitchen and the basement— were all ringing though they had their own distinctive tones. She picked up the nearest, the one in the kitchen. It was her aunt, from Delhi.

'Rohini beti?'

'Chanda mausi, hello.'

'Happy Diwali.'

Rohini was silent for a moment. She hurriedly changed the page of the kitchen calendar; it had been still showing September.

'Diwali? Oh, yes. Happy Diwali to you too.'

'You mean you didn't remember today is Diwali? Which

world do you live in?'

'Oh, one doesn't notice these things here. No firecrackers, no sweets.'

'Where is Gautum?'

'West coast, somewhere.'

'How long has he been gone?'

'About three weeks.'

'You are alone, on Diwali?'

'It doesn't matter, mausi. We are used to these things now.'

After she put down the phone, she sat quietly at the kitchen table. Was she really used to it? To being alone on Diwali? Not even a call from Gautum. Surely there must be other people, perhaps even in those houses across the field, who would be celebrating Diwali. They would have gone to the Indian shop and brought some gulab jamuns and jalebis and candles. There must be card sessions being held in houses where men and women, dressed up in silks and jewellery, would be gambling small stakes, praying for wealth and well-being. Maybe on Diwali meeting those people would actually be nice. Maybe on that day at least they would not put her off by criticizing India and everything Indian—the weather, the filth, the corruption—so much corruption, right from the airport!—and the mosquitoes, oh my God the mosquitoes ... Today if she could be with them, Gautum by her side, none of that would matter.

One was not meant to be alone on this day. One was meant to be among those one loved. She remembered that her brother would always come home on Diwali even for two days from his engineering college in Bangalore. They would play games at lighting candles along the terrace walls, five at a time, blowing off the ones that the other had lit. They would go to the Diwali mela at the Dadar Colony club and watch the display of fireworks in the tennis court lighting up the night sky. And then to the mandir, sometimes all the way to Shiv Mandir, twinkling with lights, smelling of marigolds and agarbatti.

She stared out of the window. Her aunt was right. Which world was she living in? She could grow old and die here, right in her villa under the dark green trees and nobody would know. And then they would hold an estate sale of the villa and freshly bathed weekend crowds would come, all dressed up to scavenge and go through her private life, her letters and her books, her photographs and her clothes. They would take away bits and pieces of her life in small cars, on bicycles.

Gautum returned from the west coast the day before Halloween, two days after Diwali. He spent the afternoon at home.

Rohini didn't tell me anything more. She didn't tell me if she drove to the airport to pick him up, if they kissed in the car driving back, or if they tried to make love while he struggled with his jet lag before he went off to work again. She edited all that out from her past. I learned only about the winter that followed, the winter that poisoned even her loneliness—though this was not how she told me of it. She compressed those months into three sentences:

> it was in the middle of that winter that i began to think it over, again and again, from all points of view, torturing myself over each possibility and the permutations of a hundred consequences. Spring came early that year and the sun was brighter. it was like an omen . . . and i yearned to go back home.

'I am doing all this for *us*, can't you see?' Gautum screamed, then lowered his voice to an intense growl one night when she complained that they did not have any time together any more. 'I'm not having a holiday. This is my—*our*—one big chance.'

She stared back at him, silent, distraught.

'Why don't you do something?' he continued. 'Why don't you join me in this whole thing? Take computer lessons, play the stock market, launch a business of your own.'

She wondered whether he had ever understood her.

Slowly, the anger resolved into a silent distance. He went about his life, doing what he had to do, talking to her only when it became absolutely essential. He listened to her grimly when she finally told him that she wanted to go away to India for a while. Then he said something about it being a very NRI thing to do— you come to America, you make it, then you become lonely and go back home, and three months later you are back, having got the India of your memories out of your system. She heard him in silence. Only three days before her flight did it hit him. He came back to the house, unexpectedly early at three in the afternoon. He parked the car quietly and when she walked into the bedroom she was surprised to see him sitting on the bed, his shoulders slumped, taking off his shoes.

'What happened?' she asked. 'Are you all right?'

'Yeah, I'm fine.'

'Then how come you're back home and sitting like this?'

'You are leaving me, aren't you?' he turned and looked at her. She saw tears in his eyes.

'I'm just going away for a while, Gautum. We have been discussing this for . . .'

'I know, I know.'

He lay down on the bed on his side and put his face into the pillow. She moved over to sit next to him and put a hand on his shoulder. His body heaved as he sobbed into the pillow; she couldn't see his face.

'Gautum, don't do this. You are just making it more difficult for both of us.'

He got up and went to wash his face. They sat in silence as the light faded outside the window.

'Should I get tea?' she asked and without waiting for an answer went down to the kitchen and brought hot tea in two large glass mugs.

The evening news on the television reported a tornado near Oklahoma. They stared at the screen, their thoughts elsewhere, watching clips of upturned cars, broken roofs, huge trees uprooted. Every time they showed a tornado Gautum would usually say— 'It's a terrible thing, a tornado. I survived one.' He would be referring to the tornado that went like a vicious arrow through his tech school. He had clutched a pillar in a corridor and held on as glass splintered, snapped electric cables swung dangerously, hundred-year-old trees were flung across the road and granite statues catapulted into the gaping pits where the trees had been. He had been there and guided home a helpless professor whose thick spectacles had blown off and smashed into a wall. But that evening Gautum watched the television report in silence.

She finished packing her two suitcases the night before the flight, packing them as if she was going for a long holiday. Clothes, shoes, handbags, some photographs, a few letters and a blue binder with all her degrees and testimonials. Early morning the two suitcases stood locked and labelled in the corridor. Gautum glanced at the suitcases and then at her. He didn't say anything but began to get ready.

There was time after breakfast before the flight and nothing much to do.

'Let's go for a walk,' said Rohini, keen to leave the house. If she stayed in those rooms too long, she may not go at all.

'Where? Now?'

'We can go for a while down to the canal and then to the airport straight from there.'

That was how they landed up on that bench on the banks of that canal. They sat there for a while, each trying to say something but not knowing where to start. In the end there wasn't much to say. Things seemed to have come to an end, just like the trails that petered away into the overgrown hillside above the canal. Just like that.

I feel for Gautum. Strangely, my heart pains for him. He is a kindred soul. He seems a pathetic character, innocent, until it is too late, of an impending disaster. I must have seemed like that to Jamshed and the others. And to Naini and Rajiv, who must have known almost to the second when Mina was going to pull the rug from under me. To them I must have seemed like a prize sucker. If I ever get another chance, I will somehow get even. I wonder how I will do it though—perhaps stuff silk scarves down the throat of Naini's Chihuahua until it chokes, or drip indelible ink on all of Rajiv's monogrammed light pink shirts. Pink shirts! I mean, to think that my wife actually left me for a man who wears monogrammed pink shirts . . . it's so insulting that it hurts.

8

These thoughts are messy, unmanageable baggage. Too many loose ends. I would prefer clean, sharp grief to this mess. Grief as clean and no-nonsense as the cantonment neatness of the Roorkee I knew as a boy. Perhaps it has changed, perhaps not—I'm not curious enough to step on to the platform. The memories suffice. The painted white and green walls of the barracks where the jawans walked in khaki shorts or played hockey or reclined on string cots, writing letters home in the dim evening light. There is also the memory of tea with too much milk and sugar at the bus stop, sloshed quickly into a cup of thick white china and the pungent smell of fried daal with green chillies and lime, as tempting as it is inadvisable.

And always in my mind, Roorkee is linked to the improbable life of an Englishwoman, a woman called Beatrice Harrison. She played her cello in the woods to attract the nightingales and gave a radio performance that made her famous enough to be written about in a magazine where I read about her many decades later. Her sister played the violin and they were noted as good exponents of Brahms's Double Concerto. And she won the Mendelssohn prize in Berlin. The magazine that featured them when both the sisters died, quickly, one after the other, mentioned Beatrice's place of birth as Roorkee.

I wonder how she came to be born in this town, what tortures she went through while she lived here, what particular gash in the soul drove her relentlessly to her cello. Was it that she was far away from home, the country of her ancestors, a daughter of a professor in the college that taught civil engineers how to build canals on the big rivers? Was it that she had to leave the place for England in a ship to go to University or to get married in a respectable sort of way? And was she happy then? Maybe she didn't go away until she had lived out her best years in the spread-out bungalows of the canal colonies. Maybe she even married one of those engineers and travelled with him to strange places with her beloved cello, practicing all the time, even on the wild night when the water levels went out of control and began to breach the banks of the new canal. I don't know more about her, except that she obviously did not stay on forever in Roorkee. She died aged seventy-three in a place called Smallfield in England.

Smallfield. Roorkee. Perhaps it makes sense to hide in these little places. When you live in these places, die in them, your hurt and humiliation, your failures don't become ridiculous. In the romantic, old-fashioned manner of Beatrice Harrison, you can even make of them something mysterious and sublime.

I turn away from the window and try to doze off again.

HARIDWAR

1

Spring, if one could choose such things, would be a good time to die. Suddenly. With the breeze still young in the branches, the leaves still tender and bright green, the flowers still on the ground where they fell, my last sight that of fresh, young, green blades of grass.

If I die in spring, I will not have to face another summer like the one that is blazing outside now. I can feel, even in the air-conditioned train, the dry, bristling, rushing heat that comes before the sweltering, sticky, smoggy heat. I can feel the urgent need to get to a cool room and pick the sweaty shirt off my back with a thumb and middle finger as if I were picking away my own burnt skin.

Last year I got three air-conditioners installed in the house and the old cooler was put up on the roof. It was all Mina's idea before she decided to go away. I don't know if one of these days she'll come back to take the air-conditioners also. Probably she won't be that petty—Rajiv has air-conditioners in his house, if I recall correctly. I'm sure the bedroom in which they must be spending all their time nowadays, making up for lost time, is air-conditioned. It's a large room with a balcony, with coir mats on a white marble floor. At least that's how it was when I went there. I wonder if Mina has done things to it, if she has taken it over and changed it around, in accordance with her beloved

Vaastushastra. I hope she has; that would serve Rajiv right. I hope she has turned the bed around, thrown out the plants, cut the full trees in front of the house, changed all the doors that lead out of the house, replaced the Kota stone in the entrance with blue granite, told him that the antique door that separates the drawing room from the dining place will bring him bad luck . . . then he will realize what he has got into.

Let her come for the air-conditioners if she wants. I will not beg for them. I have lived without them before and I can always bring the cooler back from the roof, put in new straw mats and fill water again. It's actually better than an air-conditioner. The breeze is fresher, younger, more fragrant and there is nothing rich or arrogant about it. In the room where we started our married life, in the days when the world was young and we made love every night, sometimes twice or thrice a night, we had only a fan. A lazy gray fan with thin red lines painted on it that merged into the gray as it spun furiously over our double bed. The thought of making love twice or thrice a night frightens me now. In fact, now that she has gone, I can say it. After those early years, even thrice a week became difficult, at least for me but obviously not for her.

One of those days I met a man in office who told me that he could get me a cooler on hire from across the river, which in those days meant a cheap deal. It was a fancy sort of cooler, made to look like an air-conditioner. It looked good but didn't work too well. I spent many days on a concrete slab, trying to pretend that I understood how it worked, while Mina looked out of the shaded room and told me to be careful or I would fall down to the lawn below, to be careful or I would be electrocuted, to be careful or I would cut my hand in the stubborn fan if it suddenly decided to come alive. I remember looking at her leaning out of the window, resting her breasts on her forearms, her charcoal-black eyes glowing in the sun. That is my wife, I thought, as if I was seeing her for the first time. She is the one I am supposed to be married to now, to make happy, to make rich. I didn't think then, as I stood in the sun on the ledge, that it would all end and happiness would be reduced to a brief early memory. I did not know then that people leave each other, divide up things, take away children, empty out wardrobes and move on. Oh I suppose I knew; but I did not believe that all these things could also happen to me.

That wretched cooler never came on with anything. I have never been too good with mechanical things, with nuts and bolts and screws. Mina held that against me. Every time I picked up a hammer or a screwdriver, I could feel her gaze closely examining my every move, comparing me silently with her father whose passion it seems was to do everything himself, from fixing his car to repairing the washing machine. She even told me once how his best Saturdays were the ones that were spent oiling all the fans in the house. I could never measure up to the man and after the initial months of our marriage I even stopped trying. But the fights did not stop. Every time I chipped the wall trying to put in a nail or cut my hand while trying to fix a plug, we would fight. And one day, in sheer frustration, I took the heavy hammer and slammed it into a crystal mirror ... Anyhow I paid two months' rent for the cooler and sent it back across the river and returned to the gray-and-red fan. I would have reminded Mina of that story if she'd come back to take the air-conditioners. I know for a few minutes she would have softened and smiled, bitten her lower lip and said that actually I should be keeping all the air-conditioners. Then she would have got all tough and businesslike. Well, if she comes for them now ... Though it should have happened by now or it will be too late for this summer. The light will change.

2

I pick up a magazine from the seat pocket. It is an in-flight magazine written half in French and half in English. It is probably a magazine picked up by Vijay Singh from his flight that he forgot to take with him. I feel sad for him. It would have been the right thing to carry home and drop carelessly on the dining table in Saharanpur. Anybody—the sons, neighbours, servants—who saw that magazine would have immediately placed Vijay Singh in the perfumed world of beautiful women, seaside resorts, fashionable malls, scotch whisky on the rocks. His victory would have been complete; he would not have needed to go into details of a lonely existence in a company apartment, cooking vegetables bought from the cheaper quarters of London. I wish there was some way that I could return this magazine to him but Saharanpur has been left far behind.

I leaf through the pages desultorily, trying to see how much French I remember from a six-month course taken twenty-five years ago, taught by a bald Frenchman in white trousers tied high up on his belly, two inches of his white socks visible over thick-soled black shoes. He had a perpetually untidy and frayed look about him, as if he had a bit of fried egg still stuck to the corner of his lips, the remnant of some hastily cooked breakfast in his third-floor Kamla Nagar flat. One evening we were both embarrassed to find each other shopping for underwear in a basement. Then he made some typically French joke and the moment passed and we went up to the street and had cups of tea laced with chocolate powder from the corner bakery. I have never had tea like that again. Come to think of it, I have never had any sort of tea with a Frenchman ever again.

I begin to read an article in the middle of a page. They actually have a name for what has been happening to me, it seems. Or at least for one of the things that has been happening to me. Cyberphobia is what a professor had called it, in some seminar in a small German town in the Black Forest. The Professor had taken up what seemed my specific case and developed a theory around it. The man's idea and his ability to put my condition in less than one printed page of English, and more or less the same in French, captivated me. A cyberphobic is a person, said Professor Lotwitz, who is doing a good job but is not keeping up with all the technological and electronic developments. This person develops an all-consuming obsession with the young, virile computer whiz-kids who are shooting up the corporate ladder behind him and are then promoted over him. This development, continued old Lotwitz, warming to the theme and going to the heart of my problems, coincides with the onset of physical changes. The male, as he preferred to refer to me, starts to go bald and lose muscle tone, develops middle-aged spread and erectile dysfunction.

I put away the packet of potato chips that I had opened. Too salty and too many useless calories. I pass a carelessly gentle hand over my hair—thinning in the middle of course, though I would not have yet gone to the extent of calling it balding. And erectile dysfunction—well yes, I suppose he was right, once in a while. But Lotwitz was not going to give up just there. He went through with a scalpel into my psychological traumas, removing layer upon layer like some meticulous surgeon with penetrating blue eyes and a determined set mouth. The male then becomes depressed, insomniac, tired, complains of burnout, starts to drink and smoke heavily and, in the final phase, loses interest in sex with wife. On all those counts, I was undoubtedly the champion of cyberphobics, to be put into a glass cage and flown around the world when Lotwitz got his Nobel Prize or its virtual equivalent.

As the train settles into a steady rhythm across the plain, I read quickly what Lotwitz described as the down phase of cyberphobics, as if the rest of it so far has been cheerily uplifting. The male decides to take action to remove feelings of despair. He joins a gymnasium and starts to dress like a young man. He begins to sport young trendy clothes, like three-quarter-length trousers. (I didn't know they were called that. I always thought they were deliberately oversized shorts.) He shaves his head, combining sex appeal with the disguising of baldness and even begins to wear a sarong at home. He then starts going to a pub or to clubs with younger men. He strains his relationships with his teenage children and his menopausal wife. Then in a final descent into the circles of hell, he has an affair with a young woman, some social climber he met at the pub, and is discovered by his wife. The office comes to know. Everything, his marriage, his career, his dreams of graceful fatherhood, is destroyed. And all because he was not technologically there, up with the geeks.

Of course I could see that the situations did not exactly match. Ankur was not yet a teenager, I had not started going to the gym or wearing all those fancy young clothes and of course I had not been able to have an affair with a young woman and have Mina find out. That would have been nice, though, an altogether better way of parting. It would have given everybody a clear-cut reason and people like Jamshed would have looked at me not so much as a loser and a sucker but as a guy who could still get and bed a young woman. It would have served Mina right too for having gone and slept with Rajiv. It would have been my ultimate revenge for that remark of hers to Naini over the phone that I once overheard—that she was unsatisfied with our sex life because every time she was about to have an orgasm, she was put off by my smell. I was hurt by that deeply and the only way that could have been completely wiped out would have been by showing her that another woman liked me, smell and all, and found pleasure in being with me. Didn't quite happen that way, of course.

I didn't carry on in my computer education long enough, that is true. I cannot download music, I cannot set up websites, I do not know or care what html stands for. Rajiv was always good at it but what the hell, that surely does not matter. Mina preferred him because he could fuck her better, not because he can design a web page.

But I can understand why Basu always smiled at me indulgently whenever he saw me staring at my computer screen, why Joy helpfully left website addresses which I should know on discreet yellow slips. I can see why my trousers rolled over my belt, why slowly, but surely, Basu began to win.

I saw it first in the confident way that he began to walk past my cabin, not glancing inside, not even peeping in to say Hullo from the door as he sometimes used to, with only his fat jowled face inside my door as if stepping inside would pollute him. And of course he no longer dropped in to have a cup of coffee. He used to do that once, about a year ago. Drop by after lunch, pull out a Dunhill cigarette, try to read all the papers on my desk upside down, glance at my magazines, probably trying to check out whether there were any foreign subscriptions and generally trying to be friendly. Then while we waited for the coffee to drip into the glass carafe, while we waited for the aroma to rise and fill the cabin, we would exchange slightly constrained pleasantries. Those were pleasantries exchanged between two grown-up men, men who did not need to kid each other, men who knew that in order to survive they may one day have to stab each other and would do so, without much compunction. Then he would have his coffee, stub out his cigarette deliberately and excruciatingly into the blue pottery ashtray on my side table, look appreciatively at himself in the mirror on the side wall, arch his eyebrows, pull in his stomach, tighten his bottom and walk out of my cabin, leaving me to open the window, chuck out the cigarette butt, pick up his coffee cup and straighten his chair. At that time we were still eyeing each other, sizing each other up, the challenger in red tie and cigarette in hand, stomach sucked in, in the right corner. The champ, middle-aged, old thin silk tie, graying, reading spectacles in shirt pocket in the left corner. But that was a year and something ago, when I really thought that most of Basu was tolerable, when I knew nothing of Neeta and what he had done to his wife and when I had not met his son, a boy like Ankur. I had even thought then that the two boys should get together, talk, play tennis, exchange notes, send e-mails to each other. Ha, that should have been great—Ankur and Basu's son exchanging e-mails. On what would they exchange notes, I wonder. How my father ditched my mother as against how my mother walked out on my father? Whose dad would be bigger? Delicious conundrum. I wonder if I had walked up to Basu, right into his cabin as he was tucking into his lunch of cilantro pesto pasta and told him about this, would he have laughed? Or would he have spluttered and fumed as I watched the sun-dried tomato burst forth from his heinous mouth and splatter his white shirt, right there at the first crease that marked the uppermost tyre of his belly?

3

I was yet to have lunch when Joy came into my cabin in her linen suit, crumpled all over in the fashionable manner of all linen suits, and closed the door behind her firmly. I was suffering what I call my twelve-thirty-ish feeling. It is caused by a sugar imbalance, Dr Rao tells me. I can feel a slight emptiness in my head, beginning at my temples and a gentle but insistent gnawing at the pit of my stomach. If I don't do anything about it till one o'clock I find myself standing up and sitting down repeatedly. Another fifteen minutes without food and I can scream at anybody who comes in front of me.

That was why I looked up with some exasperation and not a little surprise. It wasn't like her to shut the door behind her; we didn't do that sort of thing in that office. It could easily start an immediate whispering campaign all over the place, against her, against me, about the strange new things that we were starting to do behind closed doors. With a timely nudge or two from Basu it would gather all manner of spin and speed. We were fighting so hard that we didn't want anyone to hear, Joy was crying on my table, Joy was in my arms, the two of us were laughing, God help us, laughing together . . .

'There's something personal, personal for you that is,' she said. Her voice was hoarse and a little breathless, as if she had quickly walked up two flights of steps. Only that I knew she hadn't. She had come from her room; I had seen her through the glass.

'Who now?' I asked, masking my face, putting my hands on my knees.

'Don't ask me for names, all of them. I have been hearing it for a long time. But now it is becoming very critical. I have been debating for a long time whether I should tell you this. But I suppose I have some loyalty . . .'

She looked up quickly at my face, wondering if I was going to misunderstand it. I wanted to tell her: 'Go on Joy, I know it is only loyalty, the kind of loyalty that one has towards a dog or a cat. I know it is not love and don't think I am going to misunderstand anything.'

I glanced at the door. It was still shut and there were no faces peering over the glass partition.

'Do we need to shut the door?'

She ignored the remark.

'They are saying it's all wrong—on the public relations front, on the media liaison, the new projects, generally in your area. Nothing is working. They are saying you are indecisive, weak, dithering . . . all sorts of things. I'm not even sure I should be telling you all this. It's just, it's just that if you know you will be forewarned; you will be able to counter it, maybe.'

'I suppose there's no point quizzing you for details, is there?'

'I mean, I really don't know what I can say more. You have to sort it out, I suppose. Get a handle on things somehow, stop letting them just drift. Maybe take a day or two off and think about it, guard your interests.'

'It's Basu, I know. He's had it in for me all the time, what with his laugh gimmick and his slim-fast foods. Does he still have slim-fast? Or is he only on pasta again.'

'How can you go on joking about these things! That's how you get into the spots that you do. Sometimes I think you deserve to be there.'

I smiled when she said that. She had never said anything that had been more sincere or straightforward, without pretence or motive, without even a pout or touch of accent. It had come straight from the heart and I felt the hint of a strange warmth and friendship, something that I had not felt in a long time.

'Don't worry about me, Joy. First, I'm sure that things are not as bad as they seem. I know that sounds like the stupid cliché that it is; things are probably worse. But then, and I really believe this, there is a larger destiny at play here. You know the Omar Khayyam couplet about Destiny playing with all of us on a large chequerboard and then putting us back in the box when it's all done? That's what I believe in. Basu will be used for what he has to do, I will have to move or cross him or be crossed. And then one of us and ultimately both of us will go into that box. All of us end up in the box. Once you can see it that way, you can turn and go back to sleep.'

For the first time I saw Joy looking at me with unshed tears in her eyes as she clutched the edge of the table, her fingers so tightly pressed on the glass that they left marks when she finally moved her hands to reach for a neatly pressed handkerchief with several small yellow flowers and with its edge she picked at the corners of her eyes, not disturbing her mascara and yet making sure that no wayward tear had escaped.

I wanted to get up and hug her and kiss her hair and tell her to go home and think about her mother or her ex-husband or her dog or cat or her next housing instalment. Anything but me, I wanted to tell her. I wanted to whisper to her that it didn't matter to me, Joy, all this. I was already beginning to live away from it all. All this could harm me but not hurt me. I couldn't tell her all that but just to show that I was not all shaken up and because my twelve-thirty feeling was getting on to the one o' clock feeling and my headache had become more urgent, I took out my box of sugar-free biscuits and offered her some, taking two of them myself.

I didn't know how seriously to believe in Joy's fears. But the next evening, as I entered the sixth-floor bar of the Habitat Centre to celebrate Basu's fiftieth birthday, I was on the look out for all signs of perfidy despite my assumed nonchalance. Sitting along with a dozen other guests, around a huge round table under a television set on which some tennis match was being repeated, I found myself measuring every bit of his smile, following his every look, listening to every possible innuendo that may be contained in the most innocent of his remarks. But he was all charm and grace and hospitality. We drank to his health and long life from our frosted mugs of draught beer. He thanked us like some munificent God. He looks his fifty summers, I told myself, just look at the way his jaw hangs and his jowls double up and his eyebrows are almost all gone, probably shaved them off when they all turned gray. But Neeta, he still had Neeta.

'I'm so glad you all could come. I mean, a birthday party at this age! But you know Neeta. She is like that. She makes me feel young.'

Yes we all knew what Neeta was like. She made no attempt to hide what she was like. She thought she was insouciant, charming, young, dark and quite the latest rage. About fifteen years younger than Basu, though in the last few weeks I had noticed a womanliness covering her slim limbs. Sign of happiness, I had thought. I could not help feeling she was just a bit cheap and shameless, the way she had flung herself at Basu and stuck to him. Probably he still could not believe his luck and no doubt thanked God daily for having sent her to him. She had walked into his office a few months ago, aggressive and brassy, waving some strange degree on communications and media in her hand like an esoteric charm. And he had hired her almost instantly. She worked for only a couple of weeks in the company. Then she moved out of the office and into his house, right into his bedroom, which had been vacated by Mrs Basu some years ago. The story was that he still hadn't managed to divorce Mrs Basu despite his best efforts. She had gone away, I suppose she must be a sensible sort of woman, but had refused to set him free. As if that would matter with old Basu. That would matter with someone who had any character. Not with Basu. He could leave his wife and not worry. He could keep his mistress permanently and not make her his wife and not worry. Similarly, I thought with a little shudder, he could be planning my exit while offering me draught beer in a fancy restaurant and not worry.

'Let's order something ayurvedic,' Neeta was saying. 'It's got great powers for mood elevation. All those wonderful mysterious secrets of ancient Unani physicians are at our command now.'

I wondered where she had read that. Maybe like Joy she too had some favourite column that told her about cooling agents, musk elixirs, fluid iron ore, powdered mica all being added in miniscule quantities to make mutton, mushrooms, muttar-paneer more revitalizing. Perhaps that was what kept Basu going. One of those days I thought I should go and share his lunch and see if by the evening I felt that I could handle a woman like Neeta. There was something to be said in his favour; that woman did need some handling.

'We don't see you too often. Why is that?'

She was talking to me, Basu's Neeta. She was trying to be friendly, looking into my eyes with slightly forced earnestness, leaning towards me, her frizzy long hair irritating my forearm. I looked at Basu before I said something, something silly and ordinary, to her. He wasn't looking at us. His face was almost buried in the froth of beer. Somehow I felt that he had seen her begin to lean towards me and had then looked away, anticipating my glance. Then he started talking loudly, saving me from further conversation with Neeta.

'This girl, she really knows what I need,' he smiled indulgently at Neeta while all of us around the table watched this feast of love. 'She is such a sweetheart. I tell you, she went and bought the thing that I have been leching over, lusting for, all these months. A potty-putter. We are all grown-ups here so I can say it. This marvellous thing is meant for fifty-year-old golf freaks, men like me. Practice your putts while you sit on the pot. It's just the right size, the exact angle that you need. Comes with its own green carpet, two metres long, a cup at the other end and you know what, it even comes with a Do Not Disturb sign that you can hang on the bathroom door while you putt. What a treat. Thank you my darling.'

With that he leaned over and kissed Neeta loudly on the cheek, one fat hand kneading her shoulder. Across the table I felt the rush of his beer-drenched lust. It was all somewhat confusing and unexpected and I remember going down the lift with the beer jostling in my head, wondering if I should tell Joy about this cute little birthday party.

She probably came to know anyway; Joy had her ways.

4

I put away the in-flight magazine; there is danger in reading too much stuff. It makes your mind wander aimlessly in different directions. The random thoughts that come can upset everything, the carefully crafted compromises, the long-balanced decisions. They can cast a shadow on any sunlit day, start a simmering fire again somewhere in a lost corner of the heart, revive the sweet pain of youthful love, or wake one up at midnight in the cold sweat of some nameless guilt. I have made such mistakes before, as on the day I drifted aimlessly into Joy's office.

She was not there. She was gossiping away somewhere I suppose. Come to think of it now, I had taken to drifting into her office more often in those last few weeks. I picked up one of Joy's foreign newspapers from her desk. It wasn't too old. Maybe a week or ten days old and published all the way in Washington DC. I picked it up instinctively as I picked up everything that had anything to do with that faraway country, as if picking up these things would somehow bring me nearer to Rohini, help me share her days and nights.

The newspaper was open on the obituary page. I detest newspapers that have an entire page devoted to obituaries; the chance of finding, early in the morning, at least one person that you know or have heard of or have seen on the stage or have worshipped on the screen dead, is frightening. It tells me that time is running out.

Some rich philanthropist had died and left behind a great reputation as a patron of art. There were two photographs with his obit. The first one showed the philanthropist staring at a portrait of Van Dyke in one of the museums that he had helped to set up. But it was the second photograph that caught my eye. The philanthropist, a tall, heavy-set man in a fashionable dark waistcoat and coat and a wide-collared overcoat in the fifties' style, walking alongside his eighty-year-old ramrod straight father in a black overcoat and top hat. I could see thick tree trunks in the background and it seemed that they were walking in the woods on a cold gray day. I wondered what they had been talking about, father and son, the hardcore businessman father who had made all the money by working hard and making others work even harder and the son, an easy-going sophisticate, culture written all over him, waiting for a chance to hand over the hard-earned money to a line of greedy artists, museums, curators. I looked harder at the picture to see if I could make out from their faces some sign of a difference, a strain in the relationship, different ways of looking at things, a divide over money. But I found only smiles of mutual regard, an intense circle of familial warmth—in short, a good father and son relationship.

Joy came into the room just then. I knew she was staring hard at my back wondering what I was doing near her desk. She needn't have worried. I had no desire to look through her desk in her absence. I already knew what it contained. I knew where the lipsticks were, where the bag of peanuts was tucked away, where the daily perfume lay and where the bottle of the special perfume, for the special days when she was really dressed up, or going somewhere straight from office, was hidden. I even knew where the roll of peppermints was hidden, from where she took one each day and popped it into her mouth after lunch, to drive away the mustard or onion or garlic from her breath. And I knew that there was a stack of photographs at the back of the drawer, from which, every week, poor old sentimental Joy would choose one and put it in the frame on her desk. This week she had put a photograph of herself in a long yellow sweater over tight blue slacks in an autumnal forest. That must have been taken years ago. At least I couldn't remember her ever looking like that. Or maybe she looked like that when she was away from office, on holiday. Or maybe I had never looked hard enough. This weekly change of photo was her way of breaking her boredom, of having a change of scene, of almost, through that single free-choice act, taking an entire vacation. It kept her going, I suppose, and that was fine with me. She could keep shuffling those photos forever like a pack of tarot cards for all I cared, as long as she came to office, made my coffee and did not collapse in tears on the other side of my desk.

'Where did you get this newspaper?' I asked to end the scene and move out and let her come in. 'It's only about a week old. We don't subscribe to it, do we? Old Basu will have a heart attack if he finds out that the company subscribes to a foreign newspaper.'

Joy mumbled something about a friend in the airlines. Some air hostess, I presumed, who had the habit of keeping away the best newspapers and magazines—*Garden and Home*, *Cosmopolitan*, the *Traveller*, the *Geographic*—in the galley and smuggling them out, sending them occasionally to Joy, knowing of course of her interest in the latest things happening in the White House or on Broadway. I nodded understandingly and moved out of her room, away from her territory. But even as I walked away and sat down at my desk and began to work, that father and son photograph haunted me. I wanted to be that father talking to Ankur along the sea wall in Bombay or down the lawns that line the twin canals on Rajpath or in the twisting trails of the old mountains, stepping carefully over mossy rocks and bending under dripping rhododendrons. Yes, I especially wanted to take Ankur into the mountains and talk to him. Make him smell the fresh damp of the pine needles and measure the slopes that I have climbed as a child and see the eternal white peaks across the valley that still haunt me. And then I wanted to be the son, walking beside my father in the valley, in the field opposite my school with the shoulder-high grass, on the green lawns of Race Course, in bed under a satin quilt in winter beside a coal fire, listening, just listening. I wondered what would have happened to me if my father had not talked to me. I wondered what would happen to Ankur if I didn't.

Who else would fill that emptiness? Would there be emptiness at all? Or would Mina fill up all the gaps and spaces?

Would she be able to tell you, Ankur, I wondered, of milky white marbles with a drop of blue and those white sweets with thin red and green lines?

It troubled me that Ankur had never really seen a marble, never felt the sheer thrill of hitting one with another or the incomparable wealth of a dozen of them in the pocket of a gray worsted school pant. He had never taken them out one by one and watched the sun split in their glassy innards. It wasn't his fault. They didn't have them any more. Or perhaps they still had them only in some small neighbourhood shops, hidden away in a forgotten shoebox not opened since the shop owner's father died. I thought I must try to get him some, I must teach him how to play or at least show him how to get down on one's haunches and stretch the middle finger of one hand back like a bow, take aim, fire and watch glass hit glass.

If I could not talk to him, I could at least write to him. Letters were almost like marbles. Few people knew about them any more. But it would take a letter to explain about marbles. I could not even imagine sending e-mails about the many-splendoured marbles of my childhood.

Dear Ankur,

Do you get any letters at all? I should have written you some, maybe once a week in all these months that you have been away. Maybe then you could have kept them in some old box and read them again when you grow up.

But we don't do these things any more. Something has cracked inside us, some discipline, some desire. We don't do it the way that Papaji, your grandfather, used to write home, to his mother and brothers and sisters, when he was transferred out of Delhi for the first time.

Every day he would write that letter around eleven o'clock. Nothing much, just a postcard saying that we were all well and that he hoped all was well in Delhi and a few more lines about the children's studies or exams or report cards and something about the changing weather. It would go by the two o'clock post and when the mail came in at three thirty, there would be a similar letter written to my father by one of his brothers. Every day, until even the postmen at both ends became friends of the family and expressed surprise with gentle smiles if on some rare day the letter did not come. I wish I had saved some of those postcards to show you. You can't even get those postcards now; the ones with the six-paise Ashok pillar green stamp that later became red and then blue as the price increased. They were never torn up or thrown away, those letters that my father received from his brothers. They were always piled up in the windowsill in one corner with the bottle of Amrutanjan balm and the thermometer in its ivory-coloured plastic case.

I wonder where those postcards finally went. I used to make fun of them those days. I used to recite them out without even reading them; they were all so similar. That's the problem with being too young. One makes fun of the wrong things. And then it's too late to make amends. Do you make fun of me? I suppose that you do, but later you will agree with many little things that I do or say. And after that maybe you will do the same things yourself.

But I started this letter to tell you about marbles. I know that you have never played with marbles or even seen them.

They were wonderful things and in their winning and losing I spent many afternoons. For three years I played marbles like there was nothing else to do. Of course my father said that anybody who played marbles could never do well in studies and for a while he was right. My favourite marble was the dudhiya, milky white with a streak of midnight blue in it like the tail of some departing comet in a cloudy sky. I was sure that there was something magical in that marble; it seemed blessed by the stars. I always won whenever I played with it. It had a truer aim, a surer path. Once, I swear, I saw it move in mid-air to hit the marble it wanted to. I know why it was magical. It was because the Baba who sold it to me blew into it in his wrinkled, bony hands before he handed it to me.

You haven't seen people like that Baba, Ankur. I don't know where they have all vanished. Died and not been replaced. Old models of people gone like the old models of cars, like that Fiat that Papaji had, the original Fiat made in the first batch in India, whose doors opened outwards from the front edge. Easier to step out for ladies in sarees, they said.

Baba was like that. He belonged to another age. He lived in a hut in a vacant plot behind the Race Course Gurudwara, near the cricket ground. I would go to that hut in the afternoons when everybody in Race Course was asleep. My cycle would bump down the stony inner road that led to the cricket ground and I always cycled fast past that old peepal tree in the middle of the ground. All the boys said that there were ghosts under the peepal tree—there were supposed to be so many ghosts in Race Course, under the peepal, in the nullah behind the houses, near the chowk at midnight . . .

I never needed to tell Baba that I was coming. He already knew it; that was part of his magic. As I lifted my cycle over the bricked water channel at the edge of the plot, the sackcloth door on the little hut would part and Baba would come out, pulling a white sack behind him with his trembling hands, his white beard quivering. He would sit down in the shade of the hut and lean against the wall of stolen bricks. Then he would bring out the bottles of marbles from the sack. And with the marbles would come the packets of sweets. The green and white striped mints or the deep red masala sweets or the plain white ones with the juicy sticky stuff in the middle. If it was early winter, those weeks between Dussehra and Diwali, different things came out of that sack. Then, along with the sweets and the marbles, there would be the firecrackers. Little boxes of chakrees with red or green or blue strips on their edges and shining pictures of the rising sun stuck on the top. Long boxes of sparklers, the plain mousy gray ones or the grainy, shiny, more expensive ones that sparkled electric white instead of yellow. Cellophane-covered larhis of little red crackers that burst fifty times with one touch of the flame. And in little square boxes, the dreaded atom bombs with a long wick folded back onto itself to give you enough time to light it and run and cup your eardrums against the shattering sound. I can tell you today that I was scared to touch those atom bombs and I envied the bigger boys, specially the fat and fair blue-eyed Romy who could put that bomb under a tin can and light the wick and watch the can fly high into the air.

Those were beautiful days and none was more beautiful than the day that I got the dudhiya out of that bag and watched Baba's eyes light up strangely as I snatched it up.

He said it would cost me ten paise, twice the price of any other marble in that sack. But he also said that it was a very special marble and he would bless it for me. I handed over the ten-paise coin and watched him cup the marble in his hands and put it near his lips. Then his hollow withered cheeks inflated until I thought his face would burst and he blew into his cupped hands until the silver hair of his beard shook with the effort.

I wonder where the dudhiya has gone; I haven't seen it for many years now. I know it was there when I got married to your mother. It was in my special box of special things, the box with the photograph of Flora Fountain and the Bombay buses. In fact I haven't even seen that box for so long. Must be somewhere in the piles of junk that are lying around locked up and packed away. Sometime I will look for it and I'll give it to you. It can be your special magic marble and you can take good care of it.

Love,

Dad

5

I packed up all of Ankur's videos and left them at Rajiv's house. I was lucky. There was nobody at home except Ganga, Rajiv's old servant who had been with him ever since I could remember. He had been there when in the early days Mina and I used to come visiting occasionally. But then he was only a thin boy in striped pyjamas brought by Rajiv's mother from the adda of Bihari boys under the flyover on the Ring Road near Maharani Bagh. He had worked hard and he had been loyal to Rajiv. He came out freshly bathed, in a clean white vest and green checked lungi, combing his hair with the thick oil shining in them, a transistor radio blaring behind him. I had caught him in his best hour, between breakfast and a late lunch, with nobody at home. He was preparing for the evening when he would be on duty, wearing Rajiv's old pants and shirt, cooking the evening meal, bringing in the drinks and the soda and the ice.

'Come in, sahib,' he said. 'My sahib and memsahib, are not in. Should I make chai? Drink?'

I looked at him, admiring his cool demeanour, the ease with which he had accepted Mina as his memsahib and the ease with which he moved from chai to drink. I wondered how long he would last with her around. It was one thing to be a sort of Jeeves to a bachelor and quite another thing to run a house with Mina in it, locking the tea leaves, measuring the rice, asking him where all the leftover chicken really went.

'No, it's all right. Just give this box to Ankur baba. Videotapes.'

'Videotapes? You shouldn't have bothered. Rajiv sahib has lots of them'

I am sure, you bastard, I wanted to say. But these are my son's old tapes, *Jungle Boy* and *Sleeping Beauty* and *The Sound of Music*. Not your sahib's corny old English comedies and third-rate Swedish pornography.

'Just give them to him anyway. He's waiting for them,' I said and left from the door, leaving him to complete his interrupted toilet.

The phone rang early the next morning, just as the news came on with the radio alarm. They were saying something about the circle of violence that had once again unleashed itself in the Middle East. I picked up the remote control, switched on the television and switched off the radio with the other hand. The phone kept ringing and I let it. I knew it was Mina. She was the only person in the whole world who knew what time my alarm rang on Saturday morning and she had obviously been waiting for the exact moment before calling me up. She knew that the one thing that I could not take, no matter how easy and soft I was, was the phone ringing too early on the weekend. Probably she wanted something and she did not want to catch me in too bad a mood. The TV showed young boys throwing stones at armed soldiers in a barren, hard-bitten landscape of brown and gray in which the only embellishments were barbed wire and sentinel posts. On the seventh or eighth ring, I picked up the phone.

'You are up?'

'I should think so.'

'Listen, I'm sorry if it's too early but I thought you would have been woken up by the radio anyway. Anyhow, I suppose you will be taking your usual Saturday nap later so doesn't matter if you are up now. Sleep isn't everything. I was up at four today and I haven't gone back to bed since.'

I could believe that and I wondered what she had done when she couldn't go back to sleep. Had she put on the light? Had that bothered Rajiv? Or had she slipped away from the bed to the other room, to ruminate and potter around or to the kitchen to eat an apple or heat a cup of milk? She was into milk these days, I knew. Lots of calcium necessary for the educated pre-menopausal woman. Or had she opened the bar and taken out a bottle of Irish cream liqueur, justifying it on the ground that it had a lot of calcium too, and poured herself a generous measure on the rocks? In the first few years of our marriage I did not mind her getting up at these odds hours. She would wake me up too and we would make love and rig up strange snacks. And we, or at least I would then sleep beyond the sounding of my alarm and go to office with a slight smarting of the eyes. Was Rajiv following the same routine or were things different the second time around? I wondered if she woke up Rajiv too to have tea or nimboopani or milk or to make love. Did she really make him work at it or told him to just lie back and enjoy himself? I switched a channel at that thought, dismissing it. Back to the news of the Middle East. An Israeli soldier was being thrown out of a window into the arms of a raging crowd.

'Why?'

'I'm worried about Ankur.'

'So what's new?'

'Shut up. We really have to think about it and do something or he's going to grow up with a major problem.'

I wanted to tell her that she should have thought about it before she decided to move first to the other bedroom and then into her lover's arms. I knew that now she was torn between being a good mother and a real woman. So I switched a channel or two and kept quiet.

'What's wrong with you?'

'Me?'

'Yes, why are you so quiet? I mean, aren't you worried about him?'

'I am, but what can I do?'

'What do you mean what can you do? Just because we are not living together . . .'

There was silence at both ends. The situation was still too new to be talked about so lightly over the telephone.

'Go on.'

'I mean, just because of us, you don't stop being his father.'

'I know that.'

'Then do something.'

'Like?'

'I mean anything that keeps you in constant touch. He needs to be with a father sometimes. He can't.'

She stopped again. I knew what was on her mind. She knew that Rajiv was not the father figure that Ankur needed. Rajiv was for her, her pleasure, her vanishing youth, her late-night snack, but for Ankur, his future, his character, his career, she needed somebody more solid, more mature, more middle-class and staidly respectable. Someone like me. It made me feel superior and saintly.

'I am his father and I know it.'

'Well you haven't done much for him lately. Do you know he's not doing well in math and not even in English—that used to be his strongest subject. He just won't make it into any college at this rate. He got a B in his essay last week. There is no place for Bs in this world, just look at the competition.'

We were on familiar territory once again. I knew this route. It wouldn't lead anywhere. Mina would work herself into a frenzy and then go back to whatever she had inscribed in her neatly written To Do list for Saturday.

'I did do something. I came to give back his videos.'

'Big deal.'

'I wrote him a letter yesterday or day before. He should be getting it.'

'What about?'

'Marbles.'

'Marbles? All you can write about is marbles? You will never understand what I mean. This is the main problem. We are never on the same wavelength. I am talking about serious business, talking to him about his studies and his future and his growing up and all you can think of is marbles. Anyway, what did you tell him about marbles?'

'Forget it. It was just drivel. You tell me what you want me to do and how.'

I hated myself for saying that. I did not have to any longer.

'Well I think we need to get together once in a while and do things together. For his sake, nothing else. I'll plan something and call you back.'

I looked in the mirror as I got up from the bed. I needed a haircut badly. My eyes were puffy and swollen and I didn't look like I had slept straight for nine hours. It must be the sugar again. I thought for a moment about what I had eaten the night before and whether it would be a good idea to test my level that morning. Two whiskies and a couple of glasses of red wine was what I could remember. I took out the glucometer and the testing pen. I inserted a needle and twisted off the round baby blue rubber cover that protected its tip. Then I took the alcohol swab and wiped the tip of the third finger of my left hand, held my breath and felt the sharp, clean jab as the needle pierced the skin, and I watched the drop of blood swell with its sweet secret.

The next Sunday, early in the morning, we all went for a picnic to Tughlaqabad. Ankur and Mina and I and Rajiv. One big happy family. Strange that he was there, but I suppose she thought that it would have been stranger if he had not been there. They picked me up and we drove out of the traffic into the thorny gravel and rock of southern Delhi. I smiled to myself. If one looked at it in a way, all that had happened was that I had gained a chauffeur and a better car. Rajiv drove his Ford Astra with pride and a quiet, sophisticated enthusiasm. Its clinically clean interior smelt of pine from the little tree in a sachet that hung from the rearview mirror. The plastic on the doors was fresh and protected and neat and the foot mats had been vacuumed. The air-conditioner was gentle but effective and the radio played old tunes on the FM channel. It was most unlike my car, the car that Ankur and Mina were used to, and I wondered if he was taking care of his other new acquisiton, my former wife, with as much fastidiousness. Taking care that she dressed well, ate well, smelt well ... Ankur held on to my arm as he and I sat at the back and every once in a while Mina turned around from the front seat to give us a quick glance. Rajiv didn't speak much and I spoke a lot. I spoke about everything, telling myself that somebody had to make a go of this thing. And after all, wasn't I there to communicate in the first place?

How this place has changed, I told them. From my days in the first standard, those early days of our first yellow house near Safdarjang hospital. Those days I went to a school where a new building was coming up, a building with shining bricks painted dark red with white outlines, a huge playing field at the back, long corridors in the basement and a brass tap in a little courtyard. A lion with the school's motto in its crown—Courage is Destiny—hung across the shiny new façade. That lion is faded now, too much sun and too much rain. The motto seemed to mock me, but this I did not tell them. I only wondered silently to myself whether my destiny would have been different if I had shown courage. Would I have been a successful financial analyst, a managing editor of a newspaper, an advertising moghul, safe and secure with a supporting, loving Rohini by my side if I had the courage to do the right thing and not a man on the run from himself, seeking solace in a faint promise, shelter in past memories?

While that building came up we studied in large canvas tents and ate food in another tent, sitting at a long wooden table. Rice and daal served by men who cooked in a kitchen with doors darkened by tight wire meshing.

'We stood in line every morning at eleven and drank milk from oversized aluminum cups,' I told Ankur. 'When the building came up and the tents were taken off, only the square brick floors of those classrooms were left on the playing field and we used them to play four corners. One day, Ankur, I will take you to see those bricked squares. I'm sure they are still there and I'm sure kids like you are still playing four corners on them. All the boys who played with me are getting old, fat, gray, bald. We are all losers now, but those days we had the world in front of us.'

Mina turned and looked at me sharply and then glanced quickly at Rajiv and looked ahead. I was enjoying this and it served Rajiv right so I carried on. I knew Ankur was listening; he had a distant look on his face as if he was trying his best to recreate the Delhi of my memories.

'There was nothing here those days, after these houses, these Andrews Ganj government flats. None of these roads and flyovers and buildings. Just cycle tracks in the bushes and fields. And over there were fields of cauliflower and cabbage and radish. You know—the little red radish that has to be eaten in the sun in winter. One never thought all of that would vanish. And for some reason there were so many brick kilns. You have never seen one I suppose. They were all around the Qutub Minar in the days when the Qutub did not have a railing on the top floor. Now of course they don't allow you to go beyond the first floor, but earlier you could go right to the top. Somebody went and jumped down from there, some heartbroken lover.'

Again Mina looked at me sharply. I wasn't supposed to be talking like that to Ankur.

'We used to go there for school picnics too. To Qutub,

Tughlaqabad, Surajkund. It was great because on that day we did not have to wear uniforms. We went in one of those buses hired from Lajpat Nagar and sang songs on the way. I'll show you the places in Tughlaqabad where we went and took photographs and then when we go home, when you come over home, I'll even show you the photographs, if I can find them.'

Tughlaqabad came suddenly, just after a turn in the road. Somehow I had expected more distance, a long drive out of Delhi through an empty space. I had not realized how much had changed, how Delhi had reached Tughlaqabad and gone beyond it. The tomb with its narrow channel of a passage stood on one side of the road, the fort on the other. Ankur ran up that passage and then stopped, daunted by the immensity of the building. I walked up, took his hand and led him into the sombre darkness. 'Let me show you the dungeons,' I said and took him to where they had been thirty years ago and five hundred years ago. They still smelt damp and their shadows still scared me. Their skeletons seemed to remember that I had been there before. I stopped Ankur from going any further into the dark.

'Are you scared?' he asked me and then laughed and heard his laughter echo down the centuries.

Rajiv and Mina did not follow us. They were walking slowly around the tomb, reading the inscriptions, giving enough time and space for father and son to be together. Rajiv was pointing out things to Mina, looking earnest and committed. Trying too hard. They need not have come with us, I thought. I could have done all this alone with my son.

'We are going to the other side,' I told them.

I had to show him a few more things. I wanted to get away from both of them, from their suffocating small talk. So we went back down the narrow passage, crossed the road, walked around the tourist buses that waited there and began to climb the steep road up to the fort. There I pointed out to Ankur the graffiti that thousands of people had inscribed through the centuries. Dates and names of lovers were scratched all around us on ancient stones. Goats and cows roamed the inner chambers of the fort. The deserted ruins of a once great city surrounded us with its haunting emptiness. The walls were crumbling, the huge stones were being taken away, one by one, to the village beyond, a yellow and white mess with rusted television antennas and one blaring loudspeaker, the village of the owners of goats and cows.

Ankur would not let go of my hand. I took him to the flat piece of ground up high near the wall, pointing out the larks and the warblers flitting through the acacia and the bush. I showed him where I had sat in a group of schoolchildren so many years ago and eaten our tomato-and-cucumber sandwiches and had our orange squash from flowery thermos flasks. Then somebody had suggested a game of outlaws and I was photographed with both my hands raised in the air against an ancient wall while a friend, now an executive in Texas, pointed a gun fashioned of a thorny keekar branch at my head. That underexposed photograph is lying somewhere in my mother's cupboard, in an album with old-fashioned silver corners. Nobody knew at that time that Deepak would end up as a doctor in England whose wife would jump off the fifth floor of their apartment building one evening into the bustling crowd of the street below. Or that Navin would marry and go away to Canada and be deceived and earn his degree in accountancy selling hamburgers. Or, for that matter, that I would someday come back to that wall with my son and my former wife and her current lover.

That is the beauty, the sordid smelly beauty of life. Nothing is as good as when it is, I told Ankur, enjoy the present always.

Enjoy the sunshine on your face or the thrill of the rain or the company of your friends and parents when you can because things vanish or change and decay. And then, for instance, if you really have to meet your old friends, the ones in the old photographs, you have to twist and plan, take long flights, contrive situations, squeeze out holidays and even then you do not always succeed.

For a long time Ankur and I walked around. I could feel his eyes always on my face; I loved the squeeze of his hand. I would never lose him to Rajiv. Not that Rajiv seemed interested in taking him away. He was sitting with Mina now in the shadow of a large rock far below us, leaning against it elegantly. He had opened a bottle of beer and the sun glinted off the dark brown glass when he raised it to his lips. Mina was talking, her hands moving. He seemed slightly bored now and I wondered if he had ever come here as a child. Probably not and thank God for that. Otherwise his memories may have competed with mine for Ankur's attention. Occasionally he nodded in Mina's direction, telling her that he was interested in what she was saying. I smiled. I was free of the obligation to nod.

That was the last time we went out together, all three of us and Ankur. It was a failure and we all knew that. The arrangement that was arrived at thereafter suited everybody, and most of all, I suspect, it suited Rajiv. Ankur would spend every Saturday with me, and Mina, if she liked, could join us.

I will not be able to meet Ankur this Saturday but I cannot help it. Maybe some other arrangement will have to be worked out now that things have changed all over again. Sometimes I wonder, Ankur, if you feel abandoned and whether you blame me for not insisting that you stay with me and not with Mina and Rajiv. But I know this is better for you. You need a proper home, not a half drunk, depressed father clinging on to his job with the skin of his teeth and now not even that. And you know that later, when you are grown up, when you go to college, when your voice breaks, when you begin to look for girls and jobs, I will be there, close to you, helping you, guiding you. You will never belong to Rajiv. That much I know.

6

I felt Joy walking around the room, felt it at the back of my neck that she wanted to say something to me. In fact she had already come and gone once without my having looked up from the desk. I didn't want to look up, didn't want to be brought back to the office. It was one of those mornings when I had received a long e-mail from Rohini and I was still lost in the magical world it had created. I felt warm inside, a young excitement had wound its thin fingers around my heart and filled it with a sweet yearning.

Joy put some coffee on the boil, slowly, taking her time. She straightened the books on the side table, the black-and-white photographs on the walls, the two chairs across my desk.

Finally, I looked up. She had done something to her hair again. I wondered for a moment why women were always doing something to their hair.

'There's something going on.'

'Again?'

'Well I suppose you think I'm paranoid or something.'

'Far be it from me to disregard a woman's instinct. Tell me all.'

'Everybody is saying that something is about to happen.'

'You said that a month ago. After that all that has happened is that our good friend has taken me out to a fancy birthday party with his girlfriend and their famous friends.'

'There's going to be a meeting today. Do you know about that?'

'No.'

'See; you are being kept in the dark.'

And of course, Joy was right. She usually was, at least nine times out of ten.

It was a set-up, that meeting. Basu had set it up and made sure that I only knew about it at the last minute. If Joy hadn't warned me I would have been caught totally off guard. When I walked into the room at the end of the corridor, the room with the long table, I was angry and ruffled and seething, almost like Basu would have wanted me to be. He sat across the table from me, scarcely looking up, playing with his sandalwood elephant of a cufflink, the star of his Mont Blanc winking wickedly from the breast pocket of his grey-blue safari suit. He hardly spoke; I realized in a few minutes that he would hardly be speaking through that meeting. He had obviously done his speaking before, and now it was all before the Managing Director. I could see the list with sixteen serialized items drafted no doubt by Basu and left for the MD to deliver, punch by punch. Would all sixteen be aimed at me, I wondered.

They weren't. He had spread them across quite well, disguised them as large issues, important to the entire company as a whole, crucial for the corporate well-being in a fast-changing competitive environment. Administrative reforms, in brief. And if one went into the details—cuts on touring, a crackdown on long-distance telephone calls, savings on official cars and drivers, electricity (did we really have to have lights in office during the day?), overtime for Panditji for manning the lift after six in the evening—there was no limit to the absurdity that we discussed as we pushed our spoons into thick creamy pineapple pastries ordered from Wengers.

'We must also look at staffing.' The MD's voice was gruff, and even. 'I think we are overstaffed. I would like every manager to take a close look at his unit and see whether each employee is fully occupied and is worth his output.'

Basu was looking at his sandalwood elephant again. He cleared his throat and spoke.

'I think we need to look at the secretaries cadre. We have too many of them, makes us look like, like a government department. In this day and age, we should be executive-oriented, not secretary-dependant.'

I looked at him. His face was flush with smug zeal, his eyes had the shine of an evangelist. Too late I realized that he was aiming at Joy and was by implication, aiming at me. It troubled him that I had somebody, someone whom I could obviously trust, someone whom I could talk to. He wanted to hurt me by hurting her.

'Everybody has computers. Why do we need secretaries? For making our coffee? People must be laughing at us. What are we? Some sort of antediluvian brown sahibs? We have to decide whether we are going to be a profit-making competitive firm or whether we are going to become a government department.'

He spat out the last words with a vicious twist as if they described not a place where he had spent the better part of his own life but some particularly obnoxious corner of hell.

'I suppose we need to make an example,' said the MD, his eyes focussed on the papers in front of him, not wanting to reveal even with a chance glance whom he meant.

'I think that is most essential,' was Basu's instant reply. 'My secretary can be relieved or redeployed somewhere else.'

There was a moment's silence and then the rustle of paper, the scraping of chairs, the pushing back of teacups. For the moment, at least, it was over. Basu had made his point. He was the most committed, the most sincere, the most upfront, quite simply the best amongst us. The rest of us were selfish, petty, narrow-minded and not quite as aware of the larger corporate good as he was.

He walked out of the room, his shoulders slightly bowed, his gaze averted, as if the burden of the sacrifice had taken its toll on him. Others would perforce have to follow but the race was his. And so what if he had to make his own coffee.

As I saw him leave the room, I understood in a flash what he was all about, and of course it was so much like me not to have seen through him earlier. I understood his craving for being seen as disciplined, good, sincere. It had to do with Mrs Basu and the fact that she probably lay worrying in the middle of the night about her old age. It had to do with Neeta and what he must have known people thought of her. And as I understood that, my anger ebbed and a deep pity, a revolting sickly yellow pity rose up in me and showered itself all over his back as he left the room and went down the corridor.

Whispers are things I hate. They were all over the office. Little packets of evil, dipped in corporate poison, propelled by vicious hobbits, meant to kill, slowly. In the corridors, in the bathrooms, over the phone, in Panditji's lift, in the official meetings where they were scribbled on thin yellow scribble pads and shown by one evil person to another. The most vicious whispers were reserved for the smoking groups. Groups huddled in the corridor outside, handing each other cigarettes, tapping them on the back of their hands, lighting them up for each other. Twosomes or threesomes smoking conspiratorially, exchanging glances, hissing innuendoes and lies through nicotine-stained lips.

Mostly those whispers were, I was convinced, about me. I knew what formed these whispers. The latest gossip out of the Managing Director's office, the most recent spin that Basu had let out into the system about me, the latest bit that would add zest to the lunchtime existence of Joy and her friends like a touch of horseradish sharpens up a dull sandwich. I heard them in my cubicle, their sibilant swish swirled around me morning and afternoon and yet I was not party to them. I came to believe that I was whisper-resistant.

I once asked Joy about it.

'You are not the whispering type,' was her quick, pert answer.

I thought about that. Perhaps she was right. I had an instinctive understanding of what the whispering type must be like. Always at the centre of all things, the first one to get the phone calls, the one invited to every dinner, the one who can lend money without bothering about it, or take guests home to dinner without telling his wife, or stay out late, spend weekend mornings golfing with impunity, get easily into every foursome that exists—bridge, tennis, wife-swapping. If that was what it was, then Joy was right. I was not that type. As far as I could remember, I had been always left out of all exciting things, snuffed out of all conspiracies. In school I had many friends for whom I did all that was possible. And yet when it came to doing a mass bunk on a Saturday morning or coming deliberately out of uniform, wearing red T-shirts, or putting a compass point under Rita Khanna's backside just as she was about to sit down or throwing erasers under the library tables and going down after them to stare at the tiny white triangles that showed between the legs of the girls, I was not included. I always came to know about events when they had already happened. Maybe that was why it took me so long to get into that corner room in the college hostel to be part of the gang that passed the joint around and took deep drags. And that was why the boys at Sunshine Terrace had hesitated and looked sheepish and waited for my reaction when the Diceman had ruled that we should go to the red-light area to pick up a whore from a wooden cage. And that was why I was not part of Basu's bridge quartets. And of course that was the reason why I took so long to believe the reality about Mina and Rajiv.

It took a lot to be the whispering type, and I suppose it took a lot *not* to be one.

'You are too straight, you put off people by your straightness, that's really your problem,' Joy had continued, her flecked dark brown eyes looking directly into mine.

Perhaps you were right, Joy. But I am too old to change. And too tired.

The whispers of that Monday meeting when Basu pulled out his ace fluttered through the office, resting briefly on each desk. Joy stiffened as if she had been stung in the ankle by a poisonous wasp. Through the glass partition I saw her face grow anxious. Her fixed smile and even her curiosity seemed to have deserted her. She looked around, she straightened the photograph on her desk, she tapped papers absentmindedly into folders and then she caught my glance through the glass. She suddenly looked older. I signalled to her to come in.

'Coffee?' she asked as she walked into my room, the long painted nails of her right hand resting on the back of the visitor's chair.

'Why not?'

She switched on the percolator.

'I heard about the meeting,' she spoke, her voice almost a hoarse whisper.

'Mr Basu's great performance,' I responded, motioning her to sit down.

'Angela will lose her job, I suppose?'

'Seems like that.'

'What next? Or, who next?'

'Can't say.'

Joy was silent. After a couple of minutes, she jerked her head, as if she was physically dismissing away an unpleasant thought and got up to pour the coffee. No sugar for me, no milk for her. In that topsy-turvy morning of Angela's going, this knowledge itself was a comfortable bond. I noticed that as she put my cup down carefully on the coaster, her hand shook.

'You're worried?'

'Well, Angela was—is—very good. And she has been here a long time.'

That was true. The more I thought about it, the more shocking it seemed that Basu had agreed to let her go. The only thing that the company could use against Angela was her age. She could retire gracefully, she could not be fired. Her heavy voice, her authority and experience, her calligraphic handwriting on invitation cards, place cards, New Year cards, Diwali cards, were as much part of that office as Panditji's handlebar moustache.

'Will all the secretaries have to go?'

'I can't say. No point jumping the gun.'

I was trying to be careful. I did not want Joy breaking down in tears in my office. I no longer had the stomach for that sort of thing.

It all happened pretty quickly after that. Basu made a moving speech at Angela's farewell, then made his own coffee and schemed and plotted. Within two weeks, the Personnel Manager called Joy and offered her full benefits if she resigned there and then. She was also told, in a thinly veiled fashion, that if she did not resign, she would be asked to leave anyway; the management was under pressure to let extra staff go. When I saw her come into her room, pick up her photograph from her desk, begin to clean out her shelves, picking up her lipsticks, nail polish, borrowed foreign magazines in a desultory, defeated sort of way, I knew that things had ground to a dismal halt. And then something snapped.

You can spend a lifetime being comatose, a sheet pulled over your head, surviving merely by moving to the side of the road, to the spot of least resistance, and staying there, face turned away, and hating yourself for it. Years pass, and you think you are used to it, even the self-hatred ceases to matter. And then one day the light changes, the breeze shifts a little, and something that is perhaps of the least significance to you makes you turn around and walk into the middle of the road—to halt the juggernaut or be killed. Only in retrospect will you see all your life condensed in that single moment.

My mind was made up instantly. I was not going to be part of this; for once I was going to do the right thing.

'You are not leaving alone, Joy,' I told her when she came to say goodbye. 'I too have sent a note to the MD.'

'Why should *you* leave?'

'Because I feel that I must; because there is no reason for me to stay.'

I did not add that it was for the same reason that people always left places. They had to. I left Bombay and Rohini left Gautum for the same strange yearning. Mina left me, I should not forget, for the same sort of reason. And I too had to leave now. I could not see one thing, at office or at home, to hold me back.

I refused the farewell party that Basu offered, on behalf of the

MD. I handed over the office mobile telephone. I had one last cup of tea at the stall built into the wall on Barakhamba road with Panditji where he told me that within six months he too would be going away, back to his village in Bihar, and I escorted Joy to her chartered bus at the stop near Regal cinema. She was not sure what she would do; she promised to keep in touch. I told her not to take it too hard, to take care of her health. Something in her trembling hands and her quivering voice worried me.

And yes, before I left I picked up the three pages of telephone numbers and names of my friends that Joy had carefully reconstructed and tore them up. The numbers I needed I knew by heart; for the rest, I no longer felt the need to carry the burden. I was going on that sort of a journey.

7

If it had been the kumbh mela or even the ardh-kumbh, if Jupiter had been in Aquarius and the sun had entered Aries, I may have stopped here. Just picked up my duffel bag and stepped off at Haridwar. I could have become a sadhu, ash-smeared, my hair growing long in twisted ropes, smoking hashish through my cupped hands on the banks of the silver river, seeking salvation from the eternal wheel of life and death, from the senseless journey of eighty-four lakh lives. Losing count of days and nights and years, living from Kumbh to ardh-Kumbh, when ten million would come to bathe in my river in a single day. Until one day I would have joined the elements on these hallowed banks as a bag full of ash and bones, become the smoke rising thinly over the temple tops, the brilliant red tops, the white cupolas, and the crowds swaying to the chanting of the aarti. And nobody would have known. There is comfort even in that possibility; there is a strange sweetness in the thought.

A cup of tea on the platform, another short walk to stretch my legs. I stop at the A.H. Wheeler book store. It seems the books never change on these stalls, the how to books, the yoga books, the Competition Success Reviews with interviews of the toppers of the last IAS exam and the hundred sure-shot questions.

Beyond the bookstall, under the big fan outside the door of the Assistant Station Master, sits the dwarf sadhu. On a red bedsheet, wearing an oversized kurta, he rests his curved egg of a back against a huge bag. His short arm rests on his knee and he watches me, watches everyone, with red angry eyes. He is not begging but a notice on a cardboard placard next to him welcomes contributions for his akhara where the powerful wrestlers live, who need milk and almonds and pure ghee for their bodies.

What will happen if I hand him a five-rupee note? Will it help me somewhere, be chalked up in my credit in some celestial calculation? Will it give me peace?

In the afternoons the wrestlers sleep and in the evenings before the sun sinks beyond the Ganga and the lamps begin to float in the water, they twist huge wooden dumb-bells until their muscles bulge and then they fight each other in pairs, until one of them is flat out, all four corners of his back against the freshly churned soil. Such men used to come to wrestle in Race Course by the narrow canal on late Sunday afternoons, before the days of the television.

The tom-tom of the dholak, its parched leather sides being thumped by a man in a green turban and with the biggest moustache I have ever seen, from ear to ear, called across the green grass, and jumping over ditches, bouncing white flat stones on the surface of the water in the canal, sailing quick boats under the culverts, we ran to see the wrestling matches. Hands in our pockets, jiggling marbles, we watched in awe: men with muscles, bodies in tight loincloths, the oil slipping over their shoulder muscles, the quick dip to touch the earth before entering the akhara, the mutterings under the breath, the snatch and the dive and the push and the heave. And after the shouting, the winning and losing, the wrestlers having turned into ordinary short-haired men in shirts and pants, our twilight walk home, through the reluctantly dispersing crowd, to mothers leaning on the gate, glancing nervously at the light, watching the lights of Mussoorie come on, one by one, and then all at once.

I give the dwarf sadhu his five rupees and I reject his red-eyed reluctant look of gratitude. This is not for any celestial credit, I want to tell him, nor for any peace. It is for the lost joy and the forgotten light of those Sunday afternoons in Race Course, Dehradun.

DEHRADUN

1

This train does not whistle. If it could, it would have whistled now, announcing its task ahead, as it leaves the station and begins its steep incline, into the musty darkness of two long tunnels.

I shut my eyes. I can feel the light on my face as we emerge. It calms me, begins to take away some of the poison that has built up in my veins. The light has changed again. It is now the light of the hills, cool and dappled, always smelling of winter. Laboriously, the train climbs in long upward sweeps, along hill faces with small temples, sudden bustling bazaars below, open courtyards, lazing cyclists, radios on shop counters blaring the song of the day.

Soon, even without having to open my eyes, I know that we are out of the light and shade of the trees. We are through the hills, into the valley with its riverbeds, its fields of rice and sugarcane and its lichi trees.

Does one ever go back in time? Can one be a child again? Can I erase my past just by entering this childhood valley of mine and start afresh?

These questions are useless because it is happening to me right now. I am rising up in the saddle of my green Atlas bicycle, hired from the shop at the crossroads when I outgrew my blue-and-white Armour. Hired when it is still new, the red and blue and yellow decorations that always move the wrong way still bright on the hubs of the wheels. The brakes are tight and quick, the gold lettering on the bar still unscratched. I force the last burst of speed out of it on the mud track that runs parallel to the canal. My shoulders hunch low over the handle. I can feel the fresh wind on my face; I can feel that Pinky is far behind, struggling to get speed out of his older cycle, inherited from his brother who has now started driving their father's Vespa scooter. He is angry at his brother, angry at me. For once I am winning easily. And nowhere, not as far as the eye can see, is there even a faint shadow of a Rajiv or a Basu or of anyone else who would be able to show me down.

We are getting further away from home. Soon it will be time for lunch and our mothers will begin to look for us, look out of windows into neighbouring plots in which the foundations have been bricked up and left, like some new archaeological find with its secrets still hidden, its dead still unmolested. They will look into the grey veranda with the sloping roof where we often play marbles, they will call to each other across the bramble that separates the houses and then they will give up and go back inside, gathering their knitting, slightly disturbed but not really worried. Like all childhoods, ours was safe. Mina was always frenetic about Ankur; she never let him be a child, at least not the kind of child who could vanish for six hours on a hired bicycle and then return with a flushed face to a warm meal.

Pinky and I do not stop till we reach the point where the sugarcane fields begin. Here the path turns off, leaving the predictability of the firm beaten dirt and moves under the mango trees, crowded with fallen leaves, occasional twigs, till it reaches the gurudwara at Ambiwallah. Here the people come on Sundays to pray in the shade of the trees for children, success, marriage, peace. Nobody goes back empty handed from that mango grove—

only, they have to know how to ask for the favour, how hard to pray.

Pinky and I sit there near the deserted shrine, the afternoon yellow and warm around us, our cycles lying on their sides behind us. He whispers to me that it was here that they had brought Manjit, his landlady's sister, the one who could not sleep at nights because some evil ghost had taken over her body. All other attempts had failed to drive out the ghost, all the beatings with the brooms, all the incense sticks, the tempting puddings and sweets, the swirling Baba who had come all the way from Doiwallah. But here Manjit had found peace and had gone back to a new life.

I open my eyes and look towards the fields where the mango grove must still be. Can I walk to the shrine, or will I need to hire a bicycle again to go there? And if I reach there now, will I be able to pray? And if I were able to pray, what would I ask for? Would I really want to undo what Time has done to me? Could I once again pick up the torn threads of domesticity with Mina—the bill-paying, clothes-washing, bread-and-eggs kind of domesticity? Would I really want my job back, even if it means that Joy could have hers? Do I really want to see Basu's smug face even once again in my life?

The near empty bed of the Rispana yawns below us, its scattered stones echoing back the rhythmic sounds of the train. Yellowing stones with no water, white stones with yellow veins, stones with pockmarks. One December, long ago, we went to Paonta to collect such stones. The excitement, the warmth of that visit returns, tingling in my veins, though its memory has faded, like an old photograph. I grasp what I still can of those colours and fix them here, on these pages, in these lines, forever, before they fade away altogether. We brought back so many such stones from the other end of the valley where the young Yamuna chooses to go in a different direction. We collected them from across the river in Paonta, where it runs quietly, they say, to let the poets work. We collected them from the place where there was no bridge but a huge barge pushed through the water by a man with a long oar, the loose end of his red turban flapping in the river breeze. Those stones lay for years on our mantelpiece, smooth and hard, became paperweights, hammers, nutcrackers . . . Mina could never understand why I fought with her every time she wanted to throw them away. She only understood other kind of stones, the rubies and the diamonds, the turquoises and the emeralds. And she understood them best when they were embedded in solid 18-karat gold.

2

I can no longer recognize the houses. There are too many of them, one next to the other. The green patches have been eaten away. This is no longer the old valley that I had wanted to reach. The plots that were marked by gray concrete markers, markers that helped one measure the strength of a football kick or the difference between four runs and six, now have little houses on them, houses with driveways ending in garages, front gates and back gates, upstairs and downstairs. The open field beyond the Police Lines has vanished. And yet as the train swings in a wide arc, I know where I am, for I recognize the last mountain that sits like a huge elephant's foot on the valley, its purple and blue shadows colouring the sunsets.

The train sighs to a halt with a mixture of fatigue and relief; there is a familiar end-of-the-line feeling. On the platform, I walk fast. I am home. I can find with an instinctive glance the narrow side gate, through which I could take out my bicycle, if I made sure that the handlebars were turned sideways. I see men in military uniforms, berets and badges, returning from leave with bedrolls and black trunks on which their names, ranks and numbers are painted in stencilled white letters. Schoolgirls coming back to hostels, spoilt from their holidays, and muscled coolies eagerly picking up their luggage. Buddhist lamas in their maroon and yellow robes climbing into white imported vans to travel on to Happy Valley.

The computerized reservation centre is new, sitting above the road uncomfortably, self-conscious about its metal-and-paint neatness. The rest, as I sit in a tonga with its strong mixed-up smell of the horse and hay and the rain, is all the same. Clucking under his tongue, the tonga-wallah sits on the wooden bar, then stands up, gathering his dhoti in his left hand, to guide the horse past the scooters and the potholes. We turn into the unruly crowd of the bazaar.

'Laxmi Talkies?' he turns to look at me incredulously. 'What era are you talking about? Pulled down a long long time ago. It used to be a good hall. *Mere Sanam* did a hundred days, *Junglee* did five hundred.'

And so many others, some of which I saw for twenty-five paise a show, the coin slipped surreptitiously to the men who ran the projectors. Those nameless men, forever in the shadows, behind the square holes through which the film filtered out in yellow beams that lit up the dust in the dark hall all the way down to the screen. Our eyes glued to a spare hole, Pinky and I watched it all—three hours, and at least fifteen minutes of newsreel and trailers. Sometimes there were others there, policemen or friends of the men behind the projectors who needed to be obliged and then we would have to be satisfied with only a couple of songs, for ten paise. That was growing up, we thought—the freedom to go to a movie when one wanted; to eat aloo tikkis in the interval; to watch, from a level even higher than the balcony, Asha Parekh, Saira Banu, Mehmood and Shammi Kapoor; to come out with a heroic swagger in our walk, the songs of Rafi and Mukesh on our lips. Some brave days we would serenade, quietly and sadly, the unattainable schoolgirls, inspired by Dilip Kumar at a piano under a curving staircase. And rejected, we would arch an eyebrow in the self-pity of unrequited love like Manoj Kumar.

Laxmi Talkies is now a shopping complex. Advertisements for evening computer classes hang from the railings on the narrow verandas and a tailor occupies roughly that piece in the sky where our projectors used to be.

Scooters and three-wheelers and cars are overtaking my tonga from all sides. A young boy in a loose white shirt and blue-and-white striped pyjamas cycles up to the tonga and rides along. He knows the tonga-wallah.

'Where are you going, Race Course?' he asks him, glancing at me.

'Yes, sahib is going to Race Course.'

'Is he from Delhi? Or abroad?' Again he glances at me.

I want to tell him that I am from this town, and some years ago, if he had been around, we could have cycled together on these roads. We could have swung past the UP Roadways workshop, the old buses visible over the high yellow walls, negotiating the oil slicks that marked the road like maps of vanished worlds. I could have raced him up the lane with the giant potholes that leads to the district courts. Past the ancient banyan tree and the monkeys, souls of departed district lawyers, they say, still sitting there, always munching and looking both fierce and forlorn.

But I only smile at him. I can no longer cycle like that. Too much eating and drinking, too much of all that Dr Rao proscribed. I wonder for a moment what would have happened if I had never left Dehradun. Would I still be a diabetic or would all the cycling in the hills have staved off the dreaded disease? Without another glance, his curiosity broken by my unexpected smile, the young boy on the cycle peels off as we turn right into Race Course. Instinctively I search on my left for Pyarelal. He should be sitting in the second shop next to the flourmill, up the wooden steps, his head thrown sideways in a deceptively lazy gesture, his narrowed eyes watching everybody—the men drinking tea on the benches below the wooden steps, the traffic policeman in the white uniform standing at the crossing, the women with plastic baskets full of vegetables. He should be there, selling milk chocolates and cream rolls, white bread and hundred-gram packets of Amul butter, hot orange jalebis and dark brown gulab jamuns. It was not just a shop. It was the place where all gossip started and ended, fuelled by endless cups of tea. It was the haunt of tonga-wallahs in the mornings, the meeting point of servants in the afternoons, the corner that was actually the centre.

It was also for many months the limit till which I could go on my bicycle, for till Pyarelal's shop the world was safe, though the tonga-wallah reputed to have raped a foreigner was seen there occasionally, twisting his handlebar moustache or straightening his white turban in the rear-view mirror of some Vespa scooter.

Pyarelal was a resourceful man. He bought out the neighbouring shop, the shop owned by two brothers in starched salwar-kameez suits and sandals with upturned tips, and strange accents of the North West Frontier Province. Not that I minded that. Pinky and I had jointly concluded that their cream rolls were not half as fresh, not half as rich as Pyarelal's.

Later, over a space of carefully calculated two years, Pyarelal duped fat Amardeep of the house that his old mother had left him.

You couldn't miss Amardeep in Race Course, sitting in huge khaki shorts on the ribbon of a road that swept around the colony like the track on which horses once used to run. He was there every afternoon, in the middle of the road, and the cycles and the scooters skirted around him. There he sold Diwali crackers to me and Pinky and dozens of other children who were too young to get to the bazaar on their own, and pulled out magical boards on which for five paise per shot we could open little squares of paper and possibly get prizes from the huge brown bag behind his back—yellow plastic whistles, a black marble, a key chain with a photo of a puppy.

One day, after his mother died, Amardeep got tired of all this and bought a new three-wheeler and we watched him park it every day carefully in the patch of gravel in front of his house. It was a beautiful three-wheeler, painted yellow and black with Jai Mata Di written in white italic letters in front. It was a challenge to the tongas that took the residents of Race Course to the Clock Tower, to the railway station, to Doon Hospital or Paltan Bazaar, for who would want to be jostled around in a tonga if they could sit in that new machine for more or less the same money. It seemed to us then that Amardeep would make it really big, that he would make so much money from the three-wheeler that he would finally be able to set up an enormous shop full of Diwali firecrackers.

But we did not know what was happening all the time that the three-wheeler was parked at Pyarelal's shop every morning and evening. Pyarelal was giving Amardeep tea, with a plate of sweet cake rusks or a hot samosa with green mint chutney or, on some special days, two gulab jamuns with extra syrup. And he kept a careful account in a copy book. Two years after he had bought the three-wheeler, Amardeep looked at the account under his name and could not pay for it except by mortgaging his house to Pyarelal. It was a conspiracy, Pinky whispered to me excitedly, between Pyarelal and the tonga-wallahs threatened by the three-wheeler.

Pyarelal moved into the house where the mulberry tree hung low over the veranda steps. Amardeep went away on his three-wheeler, somewhere where he would not be accused every day of throwing away his mother's legacy for a cup of tea by groups of women who sat around in the sunlit verandas of Race Course, knitting sweaters, shelling peas or eating salted guavas cut neatly into four . . .

These memories of long ago, pleasant, easy memories—the kind that Ankur, poor child, may never have—rush back to help me out. Like a balm they begin to fill up all the painful cracks. Like anaesthesia, they take me away from the immediate present. Am I doing again what Mina always found contemptuous—living in the past? Oh who cares? She doesn't care any longer where I live—in the past, present or the hereafter. She only cares now where *she* lives—in the centre of Rajiv's heart and in the centre of his bloody bedroom, where he cannot miss her even if he tries.

3

In the evening I walk, not daring to look up directly at the hills of Mussoorie. Till tomorrow, when I must follow the twists and turns of the long road to a place I may have burdened with too much hope.

There are far too many people around me and not enough light. The roads have dissolved with the rains over the years and the potholes have grown larger. The brown mossy parapet along the East Canal is crumbling; at some points it has vanished completely, leaving only a base of fine grey gravel in its place. I walk along the canal, looking into the water.

This water used to run white and strong and we looked at it in awe from our bicycles, balancing ourselves with one foot on the parapet.

'A cow fell into it once,' Pinky told me, his tone hushed and serious. 'They couldn't get it out. Finally it got caught in the iron cages they have under the bridges and died.'

For days I dreamt of the cow caught in a swirling whirlpool of white water, being flung again and again at pointed iron stakes, its blood colouring the waters.

I walk on, my legs stretched by the slope. No nightmare hides in that water now, only pale reflections of childhood fears. The shops start earlier than I expected, they have swallowed the lichi gardens. Behind them the houses have shrunk, become even smaller than the visions I have carried of them in my head for so many years. Some of them have vanished along with their orchards and clean white walls and in their place are the flats, four to a compound. Two bedrooms, two bathrooms, a living room and a small balcony each. From most of those balconies the hills are no longer visible. I walk and wait for the yellow light that used to fall on to the dark road from Sunshine Bakery to show me the way.

Prem Raj of Sunshine Bakery is dead and so are his father and grandfather. That tall good-natured man, with a professor's square spectacles and lost air, is now a photograph on the wall. The whole world of Sunshine Bakery with its large glass bottles full of tea rusks and ridged biscuits, and freshly baked unsliced bread has collapsed while I have been away. I feel a strange comfort in this too; at last it is not I alone who has lost. I can share with Sunshine Bakery its grief; I can, when I need to, lean against its solid wall and weep.

Across the town, where the roads dip and swerve, are the hills with young pine tress, all in straight rows, leaving clear paths for the light to travel. I stood in that patch with my father once, when the tops of the trees were glowing a burning red at sunset. It was cold. I kicked a branch; he gingerly put a hand on my shoulder. My father's hand still shook; he was just beginning to come out of the long depression that had made life hell for him and for my mother for five long years. In his gentle, wavering touch that evening there was a quiet conviction that even when the day is ending there are things to look forward to. I suppose somewhere inside me something of that conviction went home. Enough, at least, to keep me just this side of absolute surrender. Otherwise I may not have had the courage to return every evening to the home where Mina had left fourteen years of my life in neat packed boxes, or the guts to leave the office before Basu succeeded in booting me out, or to answer even one of Rohini's e-mails.

Under the dark leaves of the peepal tree near the Forest Rangers college, the statue of a meditating Buddha shines. It has been painted over, its classic bronze ruined. I cannot muster up the reverence that I used to feel towards it every time bus number one driven by Shamsher Bahadur, the shrivelled Gurkha soldier turned driver, reached that point, stopping for Dr Ram Nath's children, the thin boy and his thin sister, his grey shorts too loose for his bony legs, her yellow ribbon bow too big for her tousled little head. I used to stare at that bronze figure, wondering who he was and what he meant to the people who were always there before the bus reached that crossing, people who left red and yellow petals in those peaceful hands.

My reverence is lost. Perhaps because it is not early morning, perhaps it is the new paint that has taken away the solemnity, or perhaps because I now understand better that enigmatic smile as it mocks me, the rest of the world, the lack of all meaning. As if the Buddha knew all along that one day I would be back: the awestruck child would return as the middle-aged runaway man and all the questions would still remain unanswered.

Past the Buddha, the road takes me to the memory of a girl from long ago. She used to wear a sunflower-yellow sash across her white uniform and a red belt around her waist and I could see her from afar as she walked the straight road along Parade Ground to her school with the yellow chapel. I was grown-up then, enough to be out of bus number one, responsible enough to be allowed to cycle beyond Pyarelal's teashop. Every morning at twenty-five past seven I waited, the dew still wet on the grass below my cycle tyres, the hills still blue in the early morning light above the flat roof of the Doon Club. I waited till I could see her beginning to walk down the straight road. I would begin to cycle then, from the other end of the road, slowing down gradually as I approached her, watching her, half smiling at her, hunching my shoulders over the handlebars, on occasion even riding with my hands free. Each morning I told her, in my own different ways, in the few seconds that I rode past her, that I had not forgotten that evening at all when we had talked fleetingly at the first social hosted by my school for the senior girls of her school. As the twilight had fallen on the school lawns in the sad way that it only does in boarding schools in the hills, the lights had come on in the teachers' quarters and I had seen the beautiful deep shadows reflected in her large brown eyes.

One day I stopped my cycle in front of her, my heart lurching to my mouth.

'I just want to ask you one thing and I hope you won't mind my asking,' I hurried, for anything could happen on that road. Her brother, known for the wild look in his eyes and his three straight victories in the district long-distance cycling championship, was said to carry a button knife.

She smiled, her eyes shining.

'In the September social, will you sit with me again?'

'Sure.'

'Is that a promise?'

'OK.'

I rode away madly after that, pedalling furiously all the way to school, wondering why I hadn't done that earlier. I could never show that kind of courage again. Not when I should have loved Rohini better and fought for her, not when I should have held on to Ankur and told Mina and Rajiv to go to hell.

As I stand now at that edge of Parade Ground where that long road begins, I can see rows of stalls with fruits and plants, with Tibetan handicrafts and sweaters. The vast open space of my world has been cut up and closed down and is all up for sale. And as for her, the one with the sunflower-yellow sash, it is only with an effort that I can even remember her name.

4

'Why do you always bring him destructive toys?' Mina had asked after I had opened my blue Aristocrat suitcase from that London trip.

'It's only a water pistol, I say.'

'It's a gun—that's what it is. It's all these things that make kids violent later.'

I must say that her views coincided with those of the airline staff. They had taken it out at the security check at Heathrow airport from my hand baggage and immediately asked me to step aside. Then a security man with a green anchor tattooed on his forearm had carefully put it aside and gone through the rest of my bag with measured gestures, as if afraid to accidentally set off any explosive device. Finally, convinced that there was no other evidence to indicate that I was a dangerous terrorist on the mission of my life and the gun was really a water pistol, they tagged it so that it would be given to the crew. It was thrown into the cockpit; the pilot, clearly an understanding man who had seen enough of this sort of stuff, kept it casually on a shelf, and in Delhi, a smiling air hostess handed it back to me with a cheery 'Enjoy yourself, sir.'

'It's for my son, actually.'

'Of course.'

I had given up and kept the water pistol away. It was no use arguing with Mina. She would have gone on and on and later, when her mother called, I would have had to hear the loud end of the conversation criticizing insensitive fathers, the thinly veiled innuendoes calling into question my upbringing, my psychology, my motives. When he was six, Ankur discovered the gun in a lower drawer of the study table where he had been looking for crayons and in a burst of poetic justice took it to his grandmother's house on Saturday and drenched the old woman. A furious Mina fought with me again that night, the veins in her neck tense and firm. But by then the fights had stopped mattering; they happened almost every day and mostly without reason.

Those days we had stopped understanding each other. It would have been futile to have taken her hand and made her sit down in the veranda with the traffic sounds outside and told her that I had bought that water pistol because of this large post office beyond the clock tower, where I now stand, in the blue-white light of the tube lights snugly fitted over the rectangular mirrors of the paan shops.

I had raced into this post office, my heart thumping after the fast uphill ride and the panic that had gripped me ever since we opened the thin plywood box left by Inder, the postman, that afternoon. Excitedly I had watched my mother sign a long form in her loose looped handwriting and hand over twenty-five rupees to Inder. It was a VPP package, ordered by her at my insistence a few days earlier from Jalandhar: an air pistol for twenty-five rupees, advertised on the inside back cover of the *Illustrated Weekly of India*. I had promised her that I would not aim it at my friends but use it only for target practice. I didn't tell her that I had wanted it ever since I had seen a teenager cycle away triumphantly carrying a pigeon that he had shot with such a pistol. Air guns were bad, I told her, one could end up blinding others with air guns, one could even end up in prison if one aimed it at somebody's heart or head. But an air pistol would be different, safer, good for children. She had relented, and I had mailed the order carefully in the red letterbox that hung on the back wall of Dr Sethi's house.

When Inder left, a little disappointed that we had not opened the box while he waited and chatted with us near the gate, I went to work with the back of the hammer to pull out the nails which kept the lid down. Inside, folded in layers of straw was a black toy pistol with a cork plugged into its barrel. It was the kind of pistol that could be bought anywhere for five rupees, not even half as exciting as the pistols that Amardeep had been trying to sell, the ones in which you could place little red firecrackers and shoot.

I was close to tears, angry and guilty at having wasted my mother's money. My mother could not believe that anything advertised in the *Illustrated Weekly* could turn out to be such a fraud. I chased Inder around Race Course but he had already gone away, having done his round for the day. I should have opened it there and then, I thought, before giving him the money. But it was too late; for the first time in my life—but not for the last—I had the sick feeling that I had been deceived.

'Maybe if you meet the Postmaster at the GPO, he can stop the money,' my mother said. She has always had a touching belief in the poor sad souls who are vested with bureaucratic responsibility—Postmasters, Stationmasters, Police officers, Army officers, District Collectors. For her they are all-powerful, committed, competent and the last protectors of the poor and the weak and the truthful. So I cycled up three and a half miles, using all the short cuts I knew, and reached the GPO, then a yellow unimposing building with rolled-up chick curtains and a clock on its small square tower.

The Postmaster caught my eye as I stood where the green curtain on his door parted, and more agitated than afraid, I pushed in. To me he seemed a very old man, in a light gray achkan, a fez cap on his head. His long salt-and-pepper beard reached down to where a gold chain curved into his achkan pocket. I had never seen such a distinguished and kind man. What I had expected was a very fat Inder, perhaps with a red sash and a large brass medallion across his chest and a big revolving chair. Instead I was face to face with a fine gentleman, a man who would have been more appropriate in a mushaira, reciting Urdu poetry, acknowledging praise, exchanging elegant compliments.

He smiled at me when I entered.

'What can I do for you, young man?'

I told him everything in a heaving rush and finally I put the plywood box on his table and took out the gun.

He moved back in mock fear, his thin lips parting in a smile that was all but hidden by his beard. Then he seemed to realize how deeply cheated I felt. Getting up from his desk, he came around and held me by the shoulders. His beard shook in front of my face with gentle restrained emotion.

'Young man, this is a very strange world. You have come to me hoping that I can do something. There is little that I can do, though I know that you have been truly cheated. The money would have already been entered for the credit of the company and once you have signed for the packet, we do not have much choice. But I know what you are feeling and I am glad that you came to tell me all this, that you felt that someone here should have the power to help you. There is good and bad in this world and the only hope for the good lies in sticking together and helping each other.'

Today I want to find that philosopher-bureaucrat, that Postmaster with the bearing of a Lucknow poet and I want to tell him that the good never stuck together. If they had, it would be Basu who would be without a job today. Joy and I would have been promoted and Angela would have been allowed to retire gracefully two years from now, with proper farewell parties, a gift of a cuckoo clock and sad speeches.

It is getting late. I take a last look at the GPO, dark after office hours except for the back corridor where there is the place where you can post letters with late fee and where the mail lies in brown sacks waiting to be thrown into red mail trucks. I know that because many of the letters that my father posted to his brothers, those letters that I should have kept to show to Ankur, were posted with late fee in that corridor at the back.

Tomorrow I will walk into Chakrata Road, the twisting suicide alley that can cut this town in two. I wonder if it still has all those old shops. Or have they all been bought up, expanded or split—the two chemists competing with each other, the sweet shop with the burfee that lived up to its reputation of melting in one's mouth. And the two sports shops, where I dreamt and salivated over cricket bats that I would have to oil myself with linseed oil bought from the hardware store. Several afternoons of oiling the bat and hitting an old cricket ball with it would bring to the surface its sweet spot. They don't do this any more. The salesman in Lodhi Market who sold me the treadmill also sold Ankur his first cricket bat, ready to go, no need to spend long hours messing around with linseed oil, half the pleasure of playing cricket already gone.

5

Rohini's last e-mail, the one that I received hours before I cleaned out my office drawers and shelves, deleted everything on the hard disk of my computer and tore the three pages of my reconstructed diary into tiny pieces, was long and relaxed.

> it's beautiful here and i am glad for whatever i have done.
> i have stopped thinking of right and wrong. for once i know
> i am happy.
>
> it seems to me that i have been here many times before, that
> i have looked over this valley many evenings, watching the
> sunset . . . i feel that i have walked these paths in the hills

before, stood at the hairpin bend looking down at the ruins of the old brewery, measured with my eyes the shadows that the gravestones cast in the old cemetery on camel's back road . . . maybe it is because you used to tell me so much of these places, of your walks here, your childhood vacations in these hills.

i enjoy the teaching. the girls are wonderful, the school is lovely. i have the afternoons mostly to myself and i love to spend them in the library . . . it has a semicircle of windows that have the most spectacular view of the peaks on a clear day and even if it is not clear, i like watching the clouds pile up in the valley and come up to the road below the school. in winter they tell me it snows quite often, and it stays on the ground. we are higher than the mall—thank god, more snow and fewer tourists.

i have been allotted a nice room . . . it is part of the old tower and actually has one curved wall with an old-fashioned window with a ledge, the kind, you know, out of which imprisoned princesses are supposed to peer at the bright moon, waiting for their rescuer to come charging up . . . as far as i am concerned, i feel i could stay here forever. i feel that i am at peace.

She is a teacher now, with a room of her own, in a boarding school for girls in Mussoorie with a long uphill drive and a little café near the gate, up in a corner of the hills that I can see even now. If I look closely in the evening maybe I will even be able to make out the lights of her school. She is so close to me, seven or eight hours if I walk, an hour or two by bus. Am I the one who urged her to go there, so that she could become a teacher with a room of her own, like that teacher of class four, tucked away somewhere in my memory since 1966, in that school that was once the estate of a nobleman from the hills?

That school is on the other side of the town, across Chakrata Road, among the pine trees. That part of town is the Army cantonment with neat roads lined with trees with half their trunks painted brick red and topped off with a white band that shines when the headlights of cars explore those deserted streets at night.

A long time ago, I entered that school for the first time, a new student from Delhi, a boy in white shorts and shirt, yet to acquire the grey baggy shorts that were part of the uniform. Chander, the peon from the Principal's office, led me to my class, III B, a sunny room with brown wooden desks and benches. That room still stands, though it isn't III B any more, and I wonder where that boy is, the boy who marvelled aloud as I entered that class for the first time—'Sir, sir, the new boy has a watch.' Or the teacher with the pointed moustache and Elvis hair who had said, 'Yes, he is not like you chaps; he has come from Delhi.'

Once again I have come from Delhi, but this time I have come with things that others will not envy. I have come with my middle-age worries and my high blood sugar levels. I have come holding the fragments of twenty years in my hands. I have come with a tiny flame of hope and the overwhelming fear of one who has been taught by experience not to hope. Nobody, not one of the ghosts who hang around the giant tree next to the small classroom will want to share all that with me. All that I have learnt, all that I have lost, all that I yearn for is all mine, to save, or to fling into the nearest ditch.

We sat on the cemented circle around that tree and ate parathas and mango achar and invented the game of outlaws, fresh out of our reading of Robin Hood and his Merry Men.

Around that tree I chased Gita, my flirtatious classmate who had picked up the aeroplane that I had made out of matchboxes and tinfoil from tea packets. That was where our flirtation began and ended, around that tree, and when the aeroplane broke as I finally snatched it from her hands, I saw guilt, fear and affection in her eyes. I rode out once on my cycle to Clement Town to trace her down in the big bungalow that she lived in with her father. Pinky went with me all the way. The idea appealed to his filmi soul, chasing a lady-love on a cycle, singing songs from *Mere Sanam*. We found the house, saw her father's name on a board tied with twisted pieces of wire to a gate with little wild wood roses all over it, and not knowing what to do after that, turned back for the long ride home, the sad songs of the fifteenth reel now uppermost in our minds.

The year passed, our teacher changed. A young, beautiful teacher fresh from a teaching institute walked into class four. She lived in a room in the staff quarters, just across the courtyard from the classroom.

That room is still part of the staff quarters. It must be home for some other young teacher today, much younger than I. I stop for a moment to look at those quarters. When she sent me to that room to fetch her keys, she was simply asking a nine-year-old to do a chore. A responsible, obedient, disciplined nine-year-old who sat at the back of the class because he was tall, who had improved his handwriting immensely in the six months that she had taught him, who tried always so hard to do well. When I went into the room to pick up the keys from the dressing table I was captivated by its coolness, its clean feminine, virginal smells. Her bed was in the corner, soft and neat. Her slippers lay neatly against the wall, next to a pair of white canvas shoes. Her dressing table, the old heavy wooden table with a swinging oval mirror, had all kinds of beautiful things on it—combs and brushes and powder cases and a crocheted cloth. And in the air hung the unforgettable smell of talcum powder and perfume—the smell of the nape of her neck. The smell that still comes to me like the first clutch at the heart, the first twinge of desire.

More than thirty years have passed, all the trees are tall, boundary walls have come up where there were open verandas and nobody here even remembers the maiden name of the young teacher who once lived in those staff quarters. I want to tell someone about her. I want to search her out in this town of crumbling bungalows and vanishing orchards and tell her what she did to me by sending me to her room that day, before she broke my heart by marrying Mr White.

Everything always begins there, at the beginning of things. And we never get over those beginnings. They linger, they torture us and we try, in unknown ways, to relive them, to make them come true and lead us to fairy-tale endings. But fairy tales are not meant to happen. One after another, beautiful fragrant beginnings go sour, turn ugly and die. And then there is nothing much left to do but consign all that is left to flames. Let the incandescent indiscriminating heat turn to dust what was sick and what was still alive, what was right and what was wrong. Then the dust of the past, the little sharpnel of bones that have proved too resistant, the remains of memories and emotions and promises can all be packed up in a bag and emptied into some sacred river of flowing time that carries away days and nights, months and years, birthdays and anniversaries. And when the sun rises again, when the first bird chirps from a young branch, when a new leaf sprouts, surprising itself, a fresh hope is born. A flicerking flame, dim as the first touch of pink at dawn.

The thought of meeting Rohini is such a hope. I dare not

think what my days and nights will mean after that. I dare not deceive a promise again; that is my only promise . . .

When I finally locate Mrs White I tell her of the ten lollypops that I won from her husband in a general knowledge quiz. I tell her I did not eat those lollypops. I kept them as precious booty in the box that I cannot now find, the one with pictures of the big red buses and Flora Fountain and huge empty streets and old slow-moving black cars. Not the pulsating Bombay of my days in Sunshine Terrace but a peaceful, untroubled Bombay. Inside that box were two pairs of cufflinks someone had given me, half a bottle of a cologne—with the magic words 'That Man, Paris' written on a label that had a figure of a slouching man in a trench coat and a hat, a red and silver Parker ballpoint pen, a small penknife, a ball of very tough string and of course some marbles, including the dudhiya. I put the ten lollypops into that box and hid it in the cupboard under my shirts until the ants got to them and they had to be peeled off stickily from the base of the box and thrown away.

She smiles indulgently. She is thinking of her husband, I know. She tells me that he died five years ago of a heart attack, that jolly athlete of a man who didn't have a care in this world and spent his days giving lollypops to little children and watching them roll and slip. How could such a man ever have a heart attack?

I watch her as she walks away. Her pale orange saree flutters in the afternoon wind. She is slight, shorter than I can remember. Her hair is dyed black. I see, over her shoulder, a vision of a young woman, in an off-white skirt and coat, walking across the football field to open the library in the old brick building, fair and beautiful, her dark glasses like those of Jackie Kennedy. She is climbing the steps now to her office, the Vice-principal's office, and as she reaches a bend in the staircase she turns around to wave to me once again. I yearn to recall how her perfume once clutched at my young heart.

Outside the school the air is still tangy and fresh, rising with the moist mystery of the green thickets that cover the nullah behind the school. I can still feel the thorns from the bushes that used to catch at my sweater at the shoulder, the bramble that used to stick onto my winter worsted trousers, leaving little pins that had to be picked out one by one in the school bus, going home.

Tomorrow, like the old times, I will walk up the hills again to Mussoorie. I will take the bus to Rajpur, till I reach the long uphill road with the few shops and houses, and then I will walk. I want to feel each step, I want my legs to ache, I want to stop and rest and every once in a while, look back. Look back at all I have left behind, at the valley as it falls before me, gradually fading, gradually widening to my vision, until I can see the hint of the sun glinting on water somewhere. Leave behind me the early sweeps of the track, wide enough to take the half-trucks that work in the limestone mines, gouging out white wounds in the timeless rock. Rest for a while at Halfway House, if it is still there, with its few tables, tea, sweets, film posters and children playing carom board. Climb into the freshness of the trees where they are thick along the abandoned railway track, past the school once meant for children of railway officers. Tire myself in the final stretch up the rock outcrops as my chest bursts, climbing into the bazaar with its smells of fresh milk bread and home-made milk chocolate and feel the clouds as they dampen the warm skin on my neck.

Then, after all these years, I will walk towards Rohini to see her smile, to feel the touch of her hand and share with her the view of the sunset over the ruins of the old brewery.